"I thought *A Heartbeat Away* was very well-written and was very effective in the portrayal of the personal side of war. Although the story is based on fictional characters, it tells a story that was very real to many during that time period. Moore's style is an easy and enjoyable read."
—Bob Murphy, RCM History Tours

"*A Heartbeat Away* is a poignant tale as deep and varied as the backdrop upon which it's set. Remarkable characters facing extraordinary circumstance, amidst the turmoil of the Civil War, make this story lasting and memorable. A MUST read!"
—Elizabeth Ludwig, author of *No Safe Harbor*

"S. Dionne Moore is a master storyteller whose way with words takes her readers deep into her story world. In *A Heartbeat Away*, she has outdone herself with the word pictures she paints of Civil War–time Maryland and a heroine torn between both sides of the conflict. Beth Bumgartner carries wounds of another kind than the Confederate soldier she nurses, wounds that are healed through her working an unfinished quilt her mother has given her. This is a story that needs to be read and savored."
—Pamela S. Meyers, author of *Thyme for Love* and *Love Finds You in Lake Geneva, Wisconsin*

Other books in the Quilts of Love Series

Beyond the Storm
Carolyn Zane
(October 2012)

A Wild Goose Chase Christmas
Jennifer AlLee
(November 2012)

Path of Freedom
Jennifer Hudson Taylor
(January 2013)

For Love of Eli
Loree Lough
(February 2013)

Threads of Hope
Christa Allan
(March 2013)

A Healing Heart
Angela Breidenbach
(April 2013)

Pieces of the Heart
Bonnie S. Calhoun
(June 2013)

Pattern for Romance
Carla Olson Gade
(August 2013)

Raw Edges
Sandra D. Bricker
(September 2013)

The Christmas Quilt
Vannetta Chapman
(October 2013)

Aloha Rose
Lisa Carter
(November 2013)

Tempest's Course
Lynette Sowell
(December 2013)

Scraps of Evidence
Barbara Cameron
(January 2014)

A Sky Without Stars
Linda S. Clare
(February 2014)

Maybelle in Stitches
Joyce Magnin
(March 2014)

A HEARTBEAT AWAY

Quilts of Love Series

S. Dionne Moore

Abingdon Press fiction
a novel approach to faith

Nashville, Tennessee

A Heartbeat Away

ISBN-13: 978-1-4267-5270-4

Published by Abingdon Press, P.O. Box 801, Nashville, TN 37202
www.abingdonpress.com

Published in association with WordServe Literary Agency.

Library of Congress Cataloging-in-Publication Data has been
requested.

Printed in the United States of America

1 2 3 4 5 6 7 8 9 10 / 18 17 16 15 14 13

For my beautiful daughter.
Love you to the hundredth power. So there!

Acknowledgments

Tip of the hat to RCM History Tours owner Bob Murphy for all the information he shared and the time he took to give me a private tour of the battlefield. He filled my head with the voices that became these characters.

1

September 14, 1862
Battle of South Mountain

Joe opened his eyes to darkness. A shadow moved against the semiblackness of a window and his senses screamed the warning. He jerked, gasped at the jolt of pain, and fell back. His heart pounded with fear at his weakness as his mind struggled to place where he was. Ben? Where was he? They had stayed close to each other. Too close. Ben had blamed himself when Joe had taken the minié ball in his shoulder. Joe heard his own voice as if from a great distance; his explanation to ease Ben's guilt: "We're in a war, what do you expect?"

He blinked as a vision of Ben flashed through his pounding head. He massaged his forehead, felt a hand on his shoulder, and swung to his left, rolling to avoid the contact. He fell into nothingness, slammed onto the floor. Pain took his breath.

"Joe!"

Through the waves of nausea he realized one thing—the voice was soft. Feminine. When the hands touched his shoulder, his face, he felt the softness in the fingertips, reminding him of home and gentler times.

"You're in a springhouse on our farm," the voice rushed to explain. "You were injured."

He gritted his teeth against the effort of even sitting up. Her hands left his arm, though he could hear the swish of her skirts. A flicker of light, then a touch to raise the wick and brighter light.

"Can you stand?" She went to the bed and yanked the covers back up that had twisted with him to the floor. "I'll try to help you."

"No." He spat out the word, and rocked to his knees, fighting for consciousness through every move. Why was there such searing pain? The minié ball injury? "I'll get up."

She guided him down onto the thin mattress and covered him with a quilt. He felt like a child being put down for a nap. Her fingers swiped hair from his brow, and he swallowed against a new tightness in his throat. How long had it been since he'd felt a gentle touch?

"I'll get my grandmother. Perhaps she can—"

"Stay." He exhaled hard, wanting nothing more than to feel her touch against his face again. To hear the softness of her voice.

She'd made as if to rise but settled back in the chair and into the circle of light. "Do you know who you are and what happened?"

"My shoulder. I was shot by a Yank in a skirmish. Ben . . . my brother was with me."

"He's not here. It's only you. You were brought here by . . . a group of people."

Such a lot of words. Too many for him to make sense of them all. Golden light shimmered against her dark hair and revealed a flash of darkness along her cheek. A dimple? He blinked and felt the grit in his eyes.

"Go back to sleep. It truly is the best thing for you."

"Ben . . ." He let the word linger, his mouth dry, lips stinging. He raised his hand to touch the burning spot along his mouth, but the effort was too much. The woman's voice was a whisper in his ear, his eyes too heavy to open, and he didn't want to. All he wanted was to know if his brother was safe. The woman had to know something, didn't she? Lost on a rise of pain emanating from his chest—or was it his shoulder?—the question spun away from him. Giving up the fight, he dragged air into his lungs and forced himself to relax against the waves of discomfort.

Gerta Bumgartner stood sentry over the inert form of the Confederate soldier, a position Elizabeth had seen her grandmother take many times in healing the sick and suffering. But this—this was different and they all knew it.

"His wound is bad, Grandmama," she worried aloud as she stepped into the coolness of the springhouse.

Gerta's sharp eyes, only now dimming with a fog that made it hard for her to focus, took in the dark interior of the room. Babbling along the floor, a spring ran up through the ground, paused to maintain a pool of water, then gurgled off beneath the wall and out into the bright September sunshine.

Another roar vibrated through the air. The two shared a look, each understanding and mirroring to the other the worry of cannons and charging brigades moving in their direction. The war was edging closer to them every minute.

"The fighting is fierce. The South will prevail."

Elizabeth should have been used to the shocking things Gerta said by now. It was part of the reason her grandmother stayed to herself and was no longer called on as much among the citizens of Sharpsburg. "How can you say that, Grandmama, knowing that your grandson fights for the Union?"

Gerta chuckled and wiped her hands on a linen cloth that lay across the wounded soldier's chest. "I say what I think." She shot her a mischievous grin. "Tomorrow, Bethie, I'll root for the Yanks."

Beth took in the soldier's gray complexion, his dry, bleeding lips. No shoes. His feet were cracked on top, the bottoms splotched with blisters and dirt.

"A right sad lot of men, if he's any example," Gerta said. "Did you burn the clothes and the bedding?"

"Yes." She couldn't help grimacing. She'd been forced to burn the rag of a dress she'd worn while dragging the louse-infested mattress and clothes out to the fire. Her ankle and leg ached from the work.

"I stripped him down and scrubbed him hard." Gerta pointed to a long tube hung on a leather string around his neck. "A louse trap."

Beth raised a brow. "Another one of your remedies?"

Another cackle of glee burst from her grandmother. "Can't take the credit for this one. It works, and there was plenty of his blood to bait the trap."

Beth stared at the narrow tube and decided she didn't want to know any more.

Gerta stroked the man's forehead almost as if she feared his skin would tear with the least amount of pressure. Beth had felt that tender touch before. Felt her grandmother's gentle pressure against the hollows of the eyebrows that helped relieve pressure in the head, or the massage that eased pain and relaxed taut muscles in the neck. "Tell me about the package," Gerta said.

For a moment, she couldn't fathom to what her grandmother referred; then she recalled the brown-wrapped package beside the armchair in front of the fireplace. "I haven't opened it yet."

"I can see that, girl, but where did it come from?"

"I brought it with me."

"Your mama."

She managed a stiff nod. "She wanted me to have something of home."

"Yet you haven't unwrapped it?"

Beth shrugged. "I haven't been homesick."

Gerta straightened and put a hand to her back, a grimace tightening her features. "I think I'll sit a spell. We'll need to bake more bread. As much as we can over the next few days."

"I've already started." She didn't bother to remind her grandmother that she'd said the same thing often over the last two days, ever since word of the Confederates moving into Frederick had been received.

Elizabeth followed her grandmother's brisk steps outside at a slower pace. Already the September air blew hot. A beautiful day, redolent with the rushes of gentle breezes and a mobcap of white clouds scudding along the blue sky. Yet, even the warm rays of the sun seemed restless as they stabbed through the clouds and then disappeared, only to reappear within seconds. She wondered, fancifully, if even God was nervous about the artificial white cloud capping South Mountain and the battle raging there.

She hadn't realized she'd stopped to stare until her grandmother's voice broke into her thoughts.

"There go the Roulettes."

Beth's gaze followed the bend in the road that ran in front of her grandmother's farm and led northeast to Hagerstown.

"Going to the church, no doubt."

"Aren't *you* worried, Grandmama?"

"You wanted to train as a nurse and the good Lord saw fit for those slaves to bring you your first patient." Gerta turned back toward the house. "We'll have more than we can handle if the fighting keeps up."

Not quite done with the conversation, she traced her grandmother's path into the generous kitchen. "You think they'll come this way?"

"They'll be all over the place. Harper's Ferry is a threat that they'll have to deal with."

"And you're not afraid?"

Gerta snorted. She dipped water from a bucket into a kettle and set it to heat. "I'm seventy-nine years old, sharp of tongue, and knowing more than all those Rebels and Yanks put together—"

"All of them?" Beth couldn't help the smile.

Her grandmother shot her a grin and flattened her lips like the bill of a duck. A comical, mischievous expression Beth had seen frequently on her father's mother's face, hard times or not. "Well, most of them. Goodness knows there's nothing much to fear at my age except dying and going to the wrong place, and I've had that one settled for years."

"But what if they steal or force you to leave or . . . ?" She shuddered, her mind going to the worst possible scenario.

Scooping tea leaves into her favorite cup, Gerta raised another, empty cup, eyebrows lifted in question. Beth nodded.

Gerta measured out tea leaves, her bright, dark gaze unflinching. "Nothing bad will happen, Bethie."

She pressed her lips together, the truth stinging afresh. "Already so many have died."

"And there will be many more who will need our help."

Nursing, she meant. It was the one dream that Beth had clung to in the days since leaving her parents' home to stay with her grandmother, intending to join with the Army of the Potomac and Clara Barton. A dream that had waned a bit as rumors circulated of the coming troops. But the blacks had come under cover of darkness the night before, bringing the soldier and igniting the need to be of more use than sitting and stitching or cooking.

Gerta had never been able to understand why the blacks had come to her instead of the town doc, other than her reputation for helping the ailing despite the color of their skin. The small town's doctor had southern sympathies.

Gerta slid the cup of tea toward her. Dutifully taking a sip, Beth couldn't help smiling. No one made a cup of tea like her grandmother, or maybe it was so good because it was made by someone who knew her as well as her grandmother did.

"You're limping."

She covered the sigh by blowing the air onto the tea. Her leg. Her ankle. Always a problem. "I want to help anyway."

"Your mother gave you jobs to keep your hands busy so you could rest your leg."

Beth didn't meet her grandmother's gaze. Gerta, of all people, knew exactly how much she despised being relegated to tasks that made her sit and rest. "It's not going to be a problem." She lifted her chin, pleased to see not an ounce of pity in Gerta's eyes.

"Then we should get to work."

Beth took a long sip of tea, dreading another day of baking. Perhaps her pride should be swallowed instead of the tea.

A sagging flour sack beckoned, as did the twenty something loaves of bread already baked, awaiting the inevitable hungry mouths of the enemy, whose goal must be to reach Hagerstown and join the rest of the Confederate army. They could hide the loaves. Save them for the Union troops that were even now engaging the Rebs. She hoped the enemy wouldn't decide to loot the Union-held garrison at Harper's Ferry that would take the Confederates through her grandmother's small town. Sharpsburg would be ravaged by the thieving monsters.

She feared her hopes were already dashed though, as reports of the Confederates in that part of Virginia had already filtered back, putting the townspeople in a vise of fright, hemmed in on three sides by the enemy.

Allowing herself to be carried off to a more peaceful time by the familiar work of adding water to flour to form dough and inhaling the yeasty sourdough scent, Beth did her best to blank her mind of the worries that nagged. When she finished kneading enough dough for four loaves, she began another batch, until perspiration dampened her neckline, flour dusted the front of her bodice, and her bad foot sent shards of pain shooting into her leg. She dragged up a stool and continued the work. Wiping the flour from her hands, she heaved a heavy sigh when the sticky flour mess mussed her skirts instead of the apron she should have been wearing to protect her clothes. She brushed at the mess and decided it best to let the moist flour dry before picking it off her skirt. She tied on her grand-mother's worn calico apron with the pretty stripes. The striped material would have been a little wild for her mother's taste, but it fit Gerta's personality to a *T*. The thought tugged a smile from her as she plunged her hands into another batch of warm, sticky dough.

The yard door rattled open behind her. Gerta opened and shut the door quickly. "The flies are terrible." She set a cup of tea down on the work surface. "I wanted him to drink some, but he fell asleep again." She surveyed Beth's work with a sharp eye that belied her deteriorating eyesight. "You've quite enough there. Add more flour to the sourdough for tomor-row's baking. I'll start on some pies while you rest."

Beth finished the dough, placed it in a bowl, and covered it to rise. A long line of bowls lined the work surface in front of her.

"Biscuits would be good as well. Maybe a meat pie."

"Are you going to have Harold take the milk cow, chickens, and horse to safety?"

Gerta measured out lard and turned to the flour sack. "He's driving Mrs. Knicks's cow, too, and said adding more wouldn't be a problem."

Beth sighed. At least the animals would be safe should the soldiers come their way and pillage. She'd heard stories of the damage they'd done at Frederick. Finished with the bread, Beth wiped her hands on the apron and picked up the tea she'd left mostly untouched. She tasted it and frowned.

"A pinch of cinnamon and a bit of the hot water," Gerta nodded toward the kettle, "will warm it up just fine."

Ridiculous that tea still soothed on such a warm day, but it did. She inhaled, and the rich cinnamon took her back to another time, years before. Her throat swelled shut as the memories assaulted her afresh. She stared down into the cup. A shell whizzed and shattered. Beth started, the tea splashing onto her hand, the tin mug slipped to the floor and spilled its contents.

A shout rent the air then. Beth caught her grandmother's moment of confusion before she wiped her hands down her apron and bolted toward the door. One word spat into the air that explained the sudden outburst. "Joe."

2

Beth held the candle up to see that Joe sat up in bed, eyes wide open as his voice lifted on another wail. Gerta moved past, her voice soothing, her hands placing gentle pressure against the man's shoulders, encouraging him to recline. But he broke into a series of panicked screams, body rigid, muscles bunched.

Beth set the candle on the low table and lunged forward to grasp his good arm. She wrenched it down to keep him from flailing and tearing open the wound her grandmother had just mended. She braced her body against his. His struggles forced her to grasp tighter, to join her grandmother's soft-spoken attempts to relieve him of his terror. Each shout ripped from him. Her ears rang with each scream and still she kept up the quiet reassurance until the muscles in his arms went flaccid and he sank back, his brow beaded with sweat, hair damp. Beth straightened, drawing air into her starved lungs. She glanced at her grandmother, and her mouth went dry when she saw Gerta's blood-saturated apron.

"He tore open the wound," Gerta confirmed, her fatigue showing in the whiteness of her lips. She stroked her sleeve across her brow, sweeping loosened tendrils of gray hair behind her ear.

Beth assessed what needed to be done and hurried outside as fast as her leg would allow. She yanked fresh linens from the drying line. Arms full, she entered the springhouse as Gerta lit the wick of the lantern and raised it to the hook she'd pounded into the wall the evening the slaves had delivered the wounded man. She blew out the candle.

At the foot of the cot, Beth dumped the fresh towels beside his feet. Where he'd been wide awake in the grip of his private terror, he now slept. She moved to the table where her grand-mother's scissors lay and placed them in her grandmother's soft hand. Gerta cut the edge of the material of Joe's once-clean shirt and ripped upward, laying bare his chest and the long, deep wound, slick with blood.

"I should have left him bare-chested. Waste of a good shirt." Gerta rolled a towel and pressed it against the wound.

"You had no way of knowing this would happen."

They worked over the inert form until the sun was low in the sky. Gerta's head tilted as if she listened for something. "You hear that?"

Beth caught on to what she meant. "They stopped."

Her grandmother's eyes flicked toward the small window high in the east wall.

Beth upended the buckets she'd used to haul water into the kitchen for boiling, too tired to think, the pain radiating in full fury. And still there was bread to bake. Gerta, too, moved slower than normal.

"He should sleep for a while. I worry about having him out here. If he wakes again, we might not hear him."

"And someone else might."

Gerta cut her eyes to Beth. "You worry too much. He's a man. He's shot. He's helpless."

"We'd be helping the enemy."

"If we get harassed for that, it's not us with the problem."

Certain in her reasoning, Gerta stepped quite lively toward the wagon. "I'll get Jim to help us take him inside. Take the wagon and fetch him."

"Won't Mr. Nisewander have a problem with—"

"He won't even miss him."

Frustrated at her grandmother's refusal to listen to any argument against her own ideas, Beth released a soft breath rather than the huff of annoyance that would have granted a measure of satisfaction. She decided to walk the short distance to the house, too nervous for the ride. Tension was bottled up in the pit of her stomach. More than anything, she wanted to head into Sharpsburg and gather news on what was happening. Stubborn her grandmother might be, but surely the woman would listen to reason if the troops were rumored to be heading in their direction. If Gerta had made provision for the livestock, she must be worried.

But somehow Beth doubted it. She believed there was little that rattled the old woman, a trait both awe-inspiring and frightening.

As Beth limped into the dense woods, she stepped carefully, imagining the muscles in her leg relaxing. At least moving seemed to ease the stiffness of standing in one place. The little log cabin of Mr. Nisewander's free field slave came into view. Jim seldom strayed far from Norman Nisewander, age seventy-two, and Norman's son refused to separate the faithful man from his ailing father. Every morning for as many years as she could remember, Jim went to the big house to care for and be companion to Norman, while the other Nisewander slaves, now owned by the son, worked in the fields.

The little log cabin stood proudly in that corner of the field closest to the woods, far from the house and outbuildings, but not so far that Jim couldn't be summoned should Norman need something in the night.

She raised her hand to knock and jumped when Jim's voice boomed out behind her.

"Jim's not home."

She turned, a ready smile on her face. The large man's coffee-colored skin retained few wrinkles despite his fine crop of silver hair. His dirty knees and the shovel gripped in his hand gave evidence to what he'd been doing.

"You look well, Jim."

"Won't feel so well if them Rebs have their way."

"You're a free man."

"Done begged Mr. Nisewander to let me hitch the wagon and take us on up to Mercersville. His brother's up there, ya know. But he say no, he too old to be rattling around in a wagon for all that ways."

Jim lowered his head a moment, his words softer now. "The leg giving you trouble?"

Beth felt the familiar poke at the precarious wall that retained her deeper emotions. "I've been on it a bit longer than usual." Descending the step, she put her good foot down first, relieved she did not fall, one of her worst fears. She tried to project a lighter tone. "Grandma has a wounded soldier at our place. She needs him moved into the house and wondered if you could help us."

Jim glanced away, his expression unreadable in the low light. "A real soldier? A Union man?"

She swallowed, wishing so much he hadn't asked, or that she didn't have to answer. "A Reb. A band of blacks brought him to us in the night. They were heading north from Middleton." She shrugged, repeating only what she'd learned secondhand.

"They risked their lives for a Grayback."

It seemed there had been more to the story. "They said him and his brother saved their lives, and they couldn't just leave him to die."

Jim seemed mollified by the news. He shifted his weight to his other foot, lips pooched as he scratched along his short beard. "Reckon it won't hurt none to help."

"She'll be grateful, as am I."

"Hurt bad, is he?"

She licked her lips, wishing for a cool drink. Jim set the pace at a quick trot that left her struggling to keep up. The limbs and brush clawed at her skirts as the two of them passed along the trail through the woods. She gasped when a prickly branch scratched across her burned hand, drawing blood. She dabbed at the area with her apron and let Jim get ahead of her so that she could rest. She hated weakness. Hated that her leg hindered her so much. Tears burned her eyes, but she widened her eyes and willed them away. Now was no time to feel sorry for herself. Not if she didn't want others to do the same.

Jim carried the wounded soldier like a baby at her grandmother's incessant urging not to jostle her patient. He knelt to lay the man in the front room on a thick pile of blankets her grandmother had prepared in her absence.

"Having him in here will work so much better. If we can just keep him still. Jim, if you'll bring in the cot, I'd rather have him higher. It'll make it easier to care for his needs and be much easier on Beth's leg."

She frowned at her grandmother, but Gerta didn't notice as she shifted the man's haversack against the wall and straightened up, hand to her back.

"It'll be easier on you as well," Beth felt compelled to remind her grandmother.

Gerta gave an absent nod and flapped a hand at Jim to send him on his way. He returned in minutes with the framework of the cot beneath his arm. At Gerta's direction he placed it against the wall, retrieved the bedding, then lifted the soldier onto it. Gerta crossed her arms and nodded in obvious satisfaction.

"That will do quite nicely. Thank you, Jim." When the black man had left, Gerta did a quick examination of the wound and the bandage, pressed her hand against the man's face, and nodded in silent approval. "Time will tell."

"Go to bed, Grandmama. I'll stay with him awhile."

Gerta's bright eyes swept over her from tip to toe. "You should rest as well. Elevate your leg and put some honey on your hand."

She'd forgotten the burn, but Gerta's sharp mind never forgot anything. Beth rose to fetch the honey, but her grandmother motioned her to stay put. Gerta fussed over the new scratches that covered the burn, insisting Beth sit in the rocker as she coated the area with honey. "Now," Gerta straightened, "the pain should ease somewhat."

"Rest, Grandmama," she said, trying to put a note of authority in her voice.

Gerta tilted her head as if considering. "Yes. I think you're right. There won't be much opportunity for rest if the war is to have its way."

Without her grandmother's spritely presence, darkness stretched its arm closer to Beth. She let her eyes roam over the placid form of the sleeping Rebel, no longer seeming so menacing without the uniform as a reminder. It seemed strange to have him so close. From where she sat in the rocker, Beth could see the side of his face and trace the shadows along his eyes and jaw. Hollows she had no doubt her grandmother would dearly love the chance to fill out with plenty of hot food once the danger of death had passed.

She leaned forward in the rocker, drawn to him. His stillness worried her. She'd been here before, watching someone on the edge of death. Her heart squeezed with dread. She didn't want the man to die. Confederate or not. Losing him to death would be like losing Leo all over again. If it was within her power to make this man well, she would do that, just as Gerta had vowed to help others all those years ago. Beth stared at her clasped hands, fighting the burn of tears. But the great drops of saltwater came anyway and splashed onto the stiff brown paper of the package in Beth's lap. Great dots of wetness that soaked into and swelled against the wrapping.

3

Beth started the rocker with a push of her foot. The brown packaging crinkled in the unnatural silence, foreboding when compared to the cacophony of shelling and gunfire that had bombarded them throughout the day, leaving the stench of gunpowder swirling in the air. She could feel the troops' nearness like the fetid breath of a stranger down her neck. She closed her eyes. Jedidiah might be among the Union men. Seeing him again would be worth the Confederates' raid into the North. But the next moment she changed her mind. Juxtaposed against the reports she'd heard from Frederick, seeing her brother would not be worth the pain and suffering the men were made to endure. Indeed, if Jed returned, he would return to her mama and papa, not here, to his grandmother's. Disappointment drew an agonized sigh from her lips. Yet things were as she had wanted them to be after the accident. She had wanted to be alone and away from the watchful eyes of her parents. She felt their concern, but didn't understand it. She was fine, she would not let her bad foot hinder her, and she just wanted to help others by pursuing nursing.

She stared at Joe's profile, grateful he slept soundly. Her time to pursue nursing would come. The war would move on to another location, and she'd be free to start her training.

Having the battle close would at least give her experience.

The brown package felt curiously light in her lap, a fact she'd mentally noted on many occasions when the tug of longing for home tried to take hold. She enjoyed the guessing game as to what the package held. Her mother had assured her nothing perishable had been packaged. Then what?

Stretching out to the table at her side, she slid the lantern closer. It was time to see what her mother had sent with her. The tiny knot securing the paper would need to be cut. She examined her nails and considered savoring the package a bit more by forcing herself to work the knot loose, but her fingernails were broken from the constant stream of work. Not that she minded. Not many women she knew had the leisure to grow long fingernails.

She pinched the knot between the index finger and thumb of both hands and did her best to work it loose. She squinted and turned the knot to pluck at the most prominent strand, finally able to loosen it a bit. Ripping the paper off would be so much fun, like returning to her schoolgirl days, when every rare gift was received with the knowledge that she had little time to spare for play with the contents before chores would be required of her. She'd rip the paper open and have the gift to savor as Jed worked his knot with patient solemnity. Even knowing they had probably received the same gift never dissuaded her brother from his solemn task.

Now she understood that need to savor the gift more than the need to play. There were a lot of things she understood so much better now than she did then.

Excitement battled against the spring of unexpected tears as she peeled back the brown paper, smoothed it, and only then allowed herself to peek at what lay inside.

———∞∞———

The slaves? Those ebony faces, fear visible in the glint of their dark eyes. Joe remembered the woman's frantic words as the group had shrunk against the back wall of the cellar. The big man holding the old, frail one, the one whose delusional shout had revealed their hiding place.

Ben's frown.

And then there was a forest, the blacks sliding away into darkness. Ben's frown again.

The glint of a rifle. The bark and then strike of the charge into his flesh. Joe had grabbed at his shoulder. Ben's face, his expression twisted into horror, staring at him, then his scream and a stream of words Joe did not hear. He was falling. Ben left. He was alone. His fingers slick with warmth. He held his hand up and saw the darkness spread on his palm. His fingers white against the night sky, except for the blood.

Ben?

Joe woke with a start and pain greeted him. He arched his back against its clutch and felt a soothing warm hand on his brow, then coldness. He withdrew, not understanding what it meant. Not caring. But the dream pulled at him. Gnawing like the rats that had plagued their campsites, drawn by the slops. The hand. His brother . . . ?

"Ben?"

Silence greeted the question. He forced his eyes open. Darkness surrounded him. He didn't want to be alone.

Somewhere in the back of his mind, he knew there should be others with him. Where were they? Was he dead?

A shuffle and a rustle yanked his attention. He stiffened, winced, and tried to see. When a light flared, a woman's face hovered in the circle of the bright glow for a few seconds before the wick was raised and the chimney lowered. Light spilled over him, over her, and he saw the smooth line of her jaw, the hazel eyes, more green than brown. Beautiful eyes and dark hair that caught the light and reflected the length of the glossy strands.

She smiled and he felt warm inside. The tension building in his mind eased.

"How do you feel?"

"Sore." It wasn't the word he'd been thinking, but it was the word that came out. He tried to order his thoughts, but his focus turned to the feel of her warm fingers against his forehead, then his cheek. He wanted to tell her not to quit. To touch him. It was reassurance that he was not dead. Pain pulsed in a biting wave, and he gasped and bit down against the fire that ate at his right side. He turned his head away. Maybe he was dying.

"My grandmother worked on your wound. She's good with herbs and knows lots about them. She'll be here as soon as she wakes."

He lifted his left hand, intending to clasp hers, but it felt swollen and heavy and would not obey his mind's request. He licked his lips, rough with dryness, winced when he felt a sharp stab and tasted blood. "It's me." He blew out a sigh, cross with his inability to speak what he was thinking. Why wouldn't the words in his head come out of his mouth?

"Let me get balm. You need to drink something. Can you?"

He wanted to sit up, to hold her hand and hear her voice. To be normal again. Back home with his brother and father, a humble man if not a rich one, enjoying life as he had until the war started and Sue was killed. He nodded at the woman's request even though he wanted nothing. It pleased her, for it coaxed a smile that was both soft and sweet.

"I'll be back."

She stepped into the shadows beyond the circle of light and was lost to him. Someone else was lost to him. The idea twisted and turned in his mind, but he couldn't make sense of the who or when, or even the where. He touched his leg with his left hand and felt the rough wool of trousers. He was dressed and lying down. His shoulder fanned an angry burn and he couldn't make his left hand rise to massage the pain away. Throat raw with his helplessness, he waited for the woman to return.

When he opened his eyes next, she was there, lifting his head and holding a tin cup to his lips. The liquid was cold, bitter. It hurt his throat when he swallowed and blazed a chill down to his stomach. He took another gulp, then another. Weak. "Wrong. It's me."

The woman tilted her head, her lips curved in bemusement, and Joe felt the first niggle of self-awareness. What was wrong with him that he couldn't speak right?

"Are you hungry?"

He shook his head and tried to get his heavy tongue to form what it was he wanted to say. "No dark."

She blinked, the long lashes making shadows on her cheeks. Those shadows, the lashes, reminded him of someone else, but he was too tired to bring the thought into focus.

"It is nighttime, about one in the morning."

Joe straightened his right leg, where a cramp had begun to grip the muscle. A groan escaped from his lips.

The woman leaned over his legs. "Which one?"

He grimaced and shook his head. She stepped back like a child corrected. He tried to sit up so he could work the knot out, but he could only moan his agony. When the muscle finally loosened, he gulped air. She hadn't left but stood by him, eyes full of concern. He drank in her presence and longed to be able to verbalize what he was thinking without everything coming out garbled and backward. He needed more sleep, for his head to clear, but closing his eyes meant she would leave and he didn't want that either. "Stay."

"Rest. Your body needs to heal." Her lips parted as if she had more to say, but she reached to lift the chimney. "I'll send Grandmother to you soon."

With one breath, she blew out the light and folded him into darkness again.

4

September 15, 1862

Beth could tell the night's weather by the inch-high ring of wetness around the hem of her grandmother's skirt as she came into the kitchen, arms full of produce. Onions, sweet potatoes, green tomatoes, too-young green peppers, squash that had yet to mature. She moved to relieve Gerta of her burden, her unspoken question answered by the shadow in her grandmother's expression.

"It's bad?"

"Jim stopped in on his way back from town. They are in Sharpsburg. Families are moving north, west, and east to escape what is to come."

"You think they will attack?"

"The Rebs have dug in deep, with a line of artillery along the east end of town. Lee has set up headquarters already. There is a rumor that they've captured Harper's Ferry."

They were here. In Sharpsburg. The enemy surrounded them. Familiar tendrils of fear coiled around her throat, threatening to cut off her air. "We should go, Grandmother. We can fill the wagon with—"

Gerta's frown sucked the words from her mouth. "You wanted to be a nurse. Do you think it is healthy people who seek a doctor? There will be much work to do. Many soldiers who will need you and me. We will stay."

She wanted to protest, stunned by the astuteness of her grandmother's observation. In her mind, nursing meant delivering babies or placing bandages on scraped knees. Why had she never considered worse? She, who knew what happened when poor care or no care was administered. There would be more wounds like the one Joe had, and probably worse. She closed her eyes, trying to imagine and prepare herself. The worst injury she'd ever seen was her lacerated, crushed foot, or the child who had poked himself with a pitchfork, gouging out his eye and driving a tine into his brain. He'd never been quite right as a result of the injury. And Leo's injury had been beyond any of that, just as he had been beyond hope of life long before she had tried to rescue him.

Gerta drifted toward the fireplace and the cot where Joe lay in restless slumber. She placed her hand against his skin. "He is too weak to move. The fever is coming on him, I fear."

With a swing of her arm, Beth pushed the iron bar holding the kettle over the open fire. "I'll clean his wound as soon as the water boils and cools."

Her grandmother said nothing as she laid strips of clean linen across Joe's chest. Then: "You opened your package."

Gerta's voice dragged Beth's attention back to the open bundle on the seat of her rocker where she had left it.

"Perhaps your mother forgot how much you despise sewing."

Despite the lightness of her grandmother's statement, Beth knew there was so much more to her hatred of sewing. The pieces of the pattern were already stitched together into blocks, ever-darkening triangles on a dark background. She'd flicked through all of them and the directions printed in her mother's neat, square handwriting.

"The last thing I tried to sew was the shirt for Leo." The stack of quilt blocks stabbed against the deep-down hurt of losing the little boy. She fought the emotion and set the blocks aside, renewing her commitment to put the past behind her. No more tears, no more guilt.

"God will not be blamed," Gerta said.

She jerked her head up, searching her grandmother's face. Is that what her grandmother thought she was doing? "I didn't see you attending service yesterday." The accusation left her lips before she'd had a chance to think better of it.

Gerta's sober expression never cracked. "It was not a good omission on my part, but Joe needed me here. And I think services would not have been much more than fear and talk. Not with the church so much closer to the mountains."

Someone pounded on the door. Gerta's gaze slid to Beth, then back to Joe before she stepped to the door. Beth wanted to call out to her grandmother and ask her to stop, her nerves drawn tight at the thought of what danger might be standing on the other side of the door.

Too late. Five Confederates, rumpled and ragged in their faded shirts and wool caps stood at the door, gaping at her, then at Gerta. The man in the forefront scratched at his chest with vigor. No doubt another louse infestation. It sickened her. These could be men who might have taken a shot at Jedidiah. Even killed him for all she knew, and the thought stirred her.

"Ma'am, we've come for a meal. If you've got anything to offer, we'd be grateful. Me and the boys are footsore and weary."

Beth lunged forward, hand grasping the door and yanking it open even farther. "And killing those for whom we stand."

"Beth." Gerta's hand on her sleeve became a supplication. Beth pressed her lips together to stop the trembling, the muscles in her back rigid with hot indignation.

"Meanin' no harm, ma'am, but they shoot at us, too."

"Of course we will feed you," Gerta waved her arm to indicate the porch. "We have a wounded soldier now who requires rest. If you'll take your leisure on the porch, we'll bring you bread."

"You tendin' a Reb, ma'am?"

Gerta didn't answer but shut the door and faced Beth. Hot disapproval sparked from her grandmother's gaze. "They are hurting as much, if not more, than Jedidiah. You saw Joe's condition, Elizabeth. He is underfed, weary; much of his trouble began with the condition he was in before he was shot. Would you turn away a man and have the same done to Jedidiah if he were needy?"

Shame burned Beth's neck. Gerta didn't wait for a reply and set about lifting loaves of bread, slicing tomatoes and the last of a smoked ham. "You must understand something, Beth. What the soldiers aren't allowed to have, they will take. You see how desperate they are, and it is either surrender what we have to them or have them burn our house and the outbuildings in retribution. They could take revenge on us personally . . ."

Gerta's hand stilled as she raised the knife to slice an onion, her words—and perhaps what she wasn't saying—lodging deep in Beth's understanding. She gathered the onions and butter and put them on a tray loaded with ham and bread, tomatoes and cucumbers.

"I'll fetch water for them."

"No need." Gerta lifted the tray, her gaze centering on something over Beth's shoulder. "Tend to Joe while I take care of these men."

Steam did not billow from the pot as it once had, and Beth knew the water had cooled enough to begin work on Joe's wound. She wiped perspiration from her brow with her sleeve and tied on a fresh apron before settling down in the chair beside Joe's cot. Already her grandmother had come in a dozen times to assess what she was doing and check Joe's temperature with the back of her hand.

Gerta gathered a yellow squash, the last of the morning's produce, on her way back to the kitchen. She rubbed at the skin, sloughing off the fine fuzz. "Don't forget to dab at the poultice until it loosens. Don't try to rub it off or you'll chafe the skin."

Another knock on the door yanked Gerta's attention back to the kitchen for the third time. It seemed the first group of hungry Rebels had shared their good fortune with their friends, bringing an influx of beggars to their door. Their bread supply had dwindled by half, and the produce was diminished to the one squash, a cucumber, and three tomatoes.

Joe moaned when Beth touched his bristled cheek. His skin was flushed from the creeping heat of fever. She used tepid water to bathe his forehead and arms, shuddering at the memory of the body lice that had clung to the clothes she had burned. Her grandmother had worked feverishly, bathing him in hot water and lye soap, scrubbing as hard as she dared, constantly throwing out bucket after bucket of dirty water.

Running a cloth along Joe's arm, she talked to him as she'd seen her grandmother do so many times. Soothing subjects of the weather and the crops, of apple pie dripping with sweet, caramelized juice and peaches that leaked juice down the chin with one bite. When she finished bathing his skin, she began dabbing at the poultice. Blood had mixed with the thick paste and crusted on the edges. With careful tugs and liberal dabs of the damp cloth, she worked the poultice loose. Every swipe of her rag revealed more of the wound. Her stomach clenched at the sight of the rounded, ragged flesh. She swallowed again and again, determined not to give in to nausea from the bile rising in her throat. She continued to talk, the distraction helping focus her on the task.

"How is he doing?"

Gerta's question took her by surprise, her heart galloping with the unexpected interruption.

"Lost in your own little world?" Her grandmother's finger traced the edges of the ragged flesh. "No sign of redness. I'll do another poultice to be safe."

Joe's body jerked on the cot, and he gasped and opened his eyes wide. Gerta placed a hand on his chest, her expression tense, no doubt reminded of his frightful display the night before. Joe blinked again, his gaze unfocused. He turned his head from Gerta to Beth. His mouth opened, but no words came forth and his eyes closed again.

"He was probably a strong man at one time. The war has taken its toll on his body." Gerta's mouth became a firm line. "You'll find that sick people often say things that don't make sense. But sometimes it's not the fever, sometimes it's the deep-down fears of the unknown or of the future."

Images of the days of her recovery came along with memories of the misery and helplessness she'd felt. The fear of a future alone because men seemed more interested in pitying her than loving her. What her grandmother said was true. She wondered if Gerta was preparing her for what would happen when and if the fever took hold of Joe, or just trying to jolt her somehow. Gerta's expression revealed nothing. The woman's aged hands moved slowly over Joe's wound, probing gently.

"Might be a good idea to start more bread while I'm working here. If their appetites are any indication of what to expect, we'll need every morsel." Gerta paused and wiped her bloodied fingers on a linen. "Unless you need to rest."

The statement lay between them like an unexploded shell. It always came back to her leg. Rest her leg. Don't exert herself. Be careful. She feared falling, but she feared the perception that she was incapable even more. "I've rested all morning," she snapped.

Sympathy stirred in Gerta's expression.

"I'm quite capable, Grandmother."

"It is not your capability I question."

"I am not a child."

Her grandmother's eyebrows lowered and she straightened. "I have never treated you as such."

She wanted to scoff. Her mother and father had treated her like a child. Always sending pitying looks her way, encouraging her to rest and get stronger. Not to blame herself. But at the intersection of life and love, she had careened down a path that detoured around both.

Gerta's expression, her words, were not piercing or full of accusation, they were soft, laced with a sadness that had nothing to do with pity. Remorse made her change the subject. "Are you applying another poultice?"

"It will help draw out the infection and protect the wound." Gerta's eyes snapped to Beth's. "But it has to be applied before it can work."

They stood, gazes locked. Gerta issuing a challenge that had nothing to do with Joe's wound. Beth pushed back a tendril of hair and tucked the wisp into her bun. She licked her lips and focused on Joe.

"I'll make it up right away," she turned to do so, feeling stripped by her grandmother's insight.

S. Dionne Moore

"Not without God you're not."

Beth snapped upright. She opened her mouth to protest the accusation, but nothing came out. Gerta wasn't listening anyway, shouldering by her en route to the kitchen.

She bit her tongue. It wasn't like she was shunning God, but she couldn't reconcile her injury—something done to save another—with God's will. She pressed her hand to her leg. How many times had she asked God to heal her and make her whole? The bones in her foot were crushed, her ankle broken. The pain was constant and worsened when she exerted herself, but she hated feeling different. As her friends got married, she had to force a show of happiness. Pretend it didn't matter that her future stretched out hollow and solitary.

Gerta returned long enough to pass her the poultice and give directions for its application. On one level, she listened closely to the careful directions, while her insides rolled and her conscience raged.

Another group of soldiers came by to beg a meal just after Beth finished applying the poultice to an increasingly restless Joe, pulled the rocker closer to the cot, and settled back. The aroma of mustard and onion drifted upward, strong, only slightly dulled by the bandage. She wrung a fresh cloth and sponged his skin, wondering, waiting for what would come next from the enemy who inhabited their town. A fierce hatred for the war choked her, and she closed her eyes to try to imagine the house full of sick, wounded men.

Joe moaned low in his throat and turned his head. She dabbed his forehead with the cooled water. His eyes fluttered open, unfocused. She leaned forward, and his eyes caught the motion and followed her movement, traced the lines of her face, his focus tighter.

"We just changed your bandage."

38

His tongue darted out over his lower lip, then his top lip. His mouth worked, and she leaned closer.

"Hurts."

The sound was that of an injured animal, pitiful, thin. "I'm sorry." She placed her hand on his arm and tried a smile. "You're starting into a fever. I'll be here for you as much as I can."

His chest hitched on a quick inhale. His lids slid down, hiding the green of his eyes. He gasped, held his breath, and exhaled.

"Joe?"

She slipped her hand down his arm, afraid of his vulnerability. His chest still rose and fell, but he'd slipped into unconsciousness. She set aside the rag, knowing there was little she could do for him. Her eyes skimmed his face, the hollows beneath his cheekbones. A handsome face. Despite the shell of a man that he'd become, she thought she could glimpse the youthful vigor he must have possessed at one time. Somewhere, deep in the South, he would have lived and worked and loved. A man. She glanced at the haversack in the corner, which held Joe's personal belongings. Would she be forced to sort through the precious things to find evidence of a wife or sweetheart to whom she would write a letter of regret upon his death?

Please don't let him die, too.

Her hands shook at the thought. At her audacity to pray when she had given up on miracles. Beth picked up the brown-wrapped package and pulled back the paper to reveal the dark blocks her mother had so lovingly sewn. It had startled her to see the dark border her mother had used. Black. But the square in the center of the quilt block was a beautiful shade of bright yellow-orange. She ran her finger over the soft fabric, thinking of the blood she'd seen on her grandmother's apron from Joe's wound. And the blood that surely ran from the men who would be injured. Or killed.

Raising the block to her cheek, she pressed the fabric close to her skin, fear gripping her tight. Things would never be the same.

5

*G*roans. *Horrible sounds, like an animal caught in a trap, desperate to be loose. Joe blinked, the white ceiling blinding to his tender
eyes. He turned his head as another agonized cry rent the air and
he saw a man, saw in hand, flies swarming despite the avid fanning
of a young boy. Joe licked his lips and felt the rough skin and tasted
the blood from a crack in his lower lip. He turned his head to the
other side, where a man lay stretched, a rough bandage around his
arm, soaked with blood. The flies were there too, buzzing, incessant,
relentless in their mission.*

*He wanted to sit up and drew a deep breath to prepare himself
for the task. He found leverage on the floor with his left hand, his
right arm strangely numb. Glancing down, he saw the bandage on
his right shoulder, pristine in comparison to the man beside him.
Pushing upward, he exhaled hard when a wave of dizziness set the
room into a hard spin. He gasped for air and waited for things to
settle down. He pushed himself to a sitting position and swiped at
the beads of sweat formed by his effort. Guns boomed, shells whined.*

*A glance down at his clothes—his pants were a dull gray, fading
to dirty beige. The colors yanked a memory. War. Then another. Ben.
He held his head in his hands and tried to make sense of where he
was and how he'd gotten here, wherever "here" was. Nothing made*

sense and his head pounded. He licked his lips. Another scream tore from the man lying on the waist-high table as the saw worked back and forth. Acid rose in his throat. He gulped air and lay down when every fiber of his being screamed at him to run.

Joe woke at the feel of coolness, tensed. He shivered and tried to focus on what was happening. The dream faded away like fog in the sun and he couldn't remember what it had been about, only that he had ridden the crest of it, remembering the fear.

He felt hot, hotter than he'd ever been and he tried to lift his hand to push at the thick quilt covering his body. Even the air felt warm. He never knew what drew him to stare into the corner, but a woman sat there, her head bent over a letter, her expression intent.

"What—"

Her head snapped up and the paper glided to the floor as she stood. She knelt next to the cot, her lips curving in a smile that blew wonder into his mind and body. She was beautiful. He wanted to touch her but his body would not release him from the throbbing pain to let him raise his arm.

"Do you remember me?"

Did he? He fought for focus. She seemed familiar. Her voice was soft and gentle, a sound he wished he could carry with him always. Anything to clear his mind of shooting, the constant drone of cannonading and rifle, the awful screams of torment that seemed to surround him, suck him in to a level of pain and torture he didn't want to experience. His dream. Of course. But if he'd dreamed it, then it wasn't real. But why was his shoulder hurting just like in the dream? Why was he flat on his back?

"No more."

Her eyebrows knitted in question and he knew what he said somehow hadn't made sense to her, but it made sense to him. All of it. The war.

"It would be good if you could drink something."

She didn't wait for an answer, her skirts fanning the air as she swept off toward another room. He had not the strength to turn his head and follow her path. He closed his eyes and waited for her to return, hoping she would reappear soon. He didn't want to go back to sleep or fade into the darkness that held all those memories. Come back. Talk to me. Let me forget. Make me forget . . .

———

Nothing made sense. In the haze of weariness, Beth understood a little of what was to come. Confederates had stopped throughout the day, appearing with apples in their hands from the Pipers' orchard they'd tromped through they came scurrying across the hills and valleys of the farms. A skirmish broke out right in their front yard when a Union soldier was found hiding in the barn across the street.

Beth saw everything from her window. She stood, transfixed by the authoritative yelling voices, the snap of fire, the cloud that rose over the three Confederate and the one Union soldier, obliterating the outcome. When the smoke cleared, the men headed toward Gerta's dooryard and the Union man lay still on the dirt road. A lone man. Dying or dead. And no one cared except her.

Her spine snapped straight, and she flung the package of quilt blocks onto her bed and streaked down the steps just as Gerta turned from the closed door.

"Don't let them in!"

Gerta's puzzled gaze skimmed over her.

"They just shot a man . . ." she paused, knuckles white against the railing, choking on a surge of anger.

"It's too late for that, Bethie. They've all shot someone at some point. You should know that."

She darted forward and yanked open the yard door. The Confederates lounged on the steps, their faces turned toward her. "Get out of here! Get off our porch, you lousy, no good—" She lost her voice. The men rose and parted as she lunged forward, lifting her skirts to clear the steps. She darted across the lawn.

Union blue flashed in the sunlight as she knelt beside the man's unmoving form. She turned him over, gaped at the blood, uncaring that it soaked into her skirts and stained her fingers. She imagined seeing Jedidiah's face, dreaded it, was relieved when it wasn't, then horrified at the hole in the side of his head. Bile surged upward, burning her mouth. She released his head, stuffed a fist to her mouth and bit down hard to squelch the scream.

The Confederates were there beside her, stone-faced. They said nothing. Did nothing. Beth rose to her feet, defeated. Nothing could be done for the man. It all balled together in her stomach—the deed, the senseless death, the gore, the innocence . . . Little Leo . . .

She faced the Rebs armed with a choking rage. They fell back, the one in the center motioning the other two to follow him, and they walked away, toward the Pipers' farmhouse.

A soft hand on her sleeve made her flinch, and she jerked. "Joe needs tending," Gerta's voice was a firm whisper in her ear. "There will be more coming. More death and dying, Beth."

"I can't do this."

"What about them? What toll do you think it takes on them?"

She shot a look at the departing men. "Nothing. They like it."

"That's your rage talking."

Indignation rose. "They shot him. I watched it happen. Like he was a dog—"

Gerta tugged on her arm. "Come on, Beth. I'll have Jim come and bury him. Joe needs your attention."

Joe. A Confederate. He was no better than the three men vaulting the Pipers' fence, disappearing among the apple trees.

Gerta mounted the steps before her, the familiar warmth and the smell of bread and sauerkraut meeting her upon entering the house. She glanced beyond the kitchen into the narrow parlor where Joe lay, restless, whimpers coming from his throat. She didn't want to go to him. Every ounce of desire to nurse was sapped from her. She collapsed into a chair, and cupped her head in her hands, and pressed her fingers against her temples where a dull ache had begun to form.

"They're shooting at each other, Beth, and there's nothing you or I can do to stop it. One side will win, the other will lose, but thousands upon thousands of women and men and children will forever have their lives changed because, North or South, they lost someone they loved."

"I know that."

"I don't doubt that you do, but I think it's easy to forget. To take sides because we don't like what we're seeing. These men are trained to do what they're doing. They don't have to like it—it's expected of them." Gerta touched the back of Beth's hand. Beth lifted her face and accepted the touch, closing her eyes against the burn of tears.

"I don't know if . . ."

"It's going to be worse, if I don't miss my guess. The Confederates hold the town. People are leaving. Things will be destroyed, lives, homes . . ." Gerta's expression pinched into the saddest expression Beth had ever witnessed on her face. What she saw there, in the face of the grandmother she so loved, tugged at a level where Beth rarely let her emotions go. It hurt too much to see the agony. Her anger churned into the need to run.

"I can't bear to watch this . . . carnage."

"It's not the watching you're being asked to do, it's the helping. The healing. That's what a nurse is all about."

Beth stole a glance at Joe. Beyond the gray uniform he wore when he arrived, he was a man. No more and no less. She must not lose sight of that fact.

In her school days, there'd been a boy much like the Confederates. He'd been unconcerned with others, taunting, spending more time hating others than he did learning. Being much older, Beth had kept her distance from him. Jedidiah had fallen prey to the boy's pranks, until his friend had rescued her brother. Not with his fists, for gentle Leo never fought anyone, but with his words. A boy wise beyond his seven years. Within the week, Leo would be dead in a fire and everyone would forget him. Except her. Her injury was the memory she held of him.

"If you want to leave, you can take the wagon. I fear that if the horse stays the Rebs will come for her."

"Wouldn't they have taken her by now?"

Gerta shrugged. "Perhaps not. I have been feeding them, you know."

"If our boys fight through, we could be in trouble for having helped the Rebs."

Her grandmother rose from the table. It took a full thirty seconds for her to straighten completely, yet she never once glanced in Beth's direction. "When did your faith stop and the worry take over, Bethie?"

6

Ben's laugh rang deep and loud in the close confines. Joe stared, trying to understand the reason for his brother's good humor. He scratched his chest, miserable, hungry, and ducked out of the corncrib that provided precarious shelter to stretch his legs. He wandered among the campfires lighting the night like a band of fireflies blazing their color all at once.

"We'll be moving soon," said one of the men, hovering near the fire, hands outstretched to catch the warmth in the cold night.

Joe couldn't hear his companions' reply, but he heard their raucous laughter when a soldier stood up and blazed a trail to the edge of camp. Effects of eating green corn, or bad rations. He'd seen the reaction a million times. His own stomach gurgled with the need for food, but he resisted eating just anything despite his hunger, knowing the ill effects often suffered.

He wound his way back toward the corncrib at the edge of the meadow, passing the tent of General Daniel Hill, and listened hard for whispers of what might be in store for them. His feet started to burn in the damp coolness of the meadow grass, and he stumbled toward the shelter. Ben was gone, four other soldiers crowding in, drawn by the idea of a roof and some corn left over from a previous *harvest. He unrolled his ragged blanket and folded into it, careful to put his weight on it lest another take it from him in the night.*

Ben came in much later and squatted next to him. In the darkness, he could see his brother's smile and wondered vaguely what it was that had Ben so amused. Through half-lidded eyes, he watched his brother settle down for the night. Saw him drag Joe's haversack closer. He fingered something long and slender, smiled, then slipped it into the sack. "Things are gonna get better real soon, Brother. Real soon."

Above Beth's head, the floor creaked. Gerta couldn't sleep either. An eerie quiet stretched over the house and the countryside. Beth stroked the length of the two quilt blocks she held side by side on her lap. She'd dared to light a lantern after putting a blanket over the window that looked onto the porch from the kitchen. She rocked next to where Joe lay, keeping the wick low as she worked the needle.

She wondered if Gerta's restlessness stemmed from the new wounded man out in the springhouse, fear of what was coming, or a general restlessness. As she pulled the needle through the material, she let her mind wander from the task at hand to the mental image of her mother doing the same thing. Quilt after quilt produced beneath her mother's steady hand. Beth smiled at her impatience with the task. She'd had no desire to sit and sew, especially when the task was pushed on her because it helped "rest" her leg. None of her mother's knack for putting together colors and following patterns flowed in her blood. Yet here she sat, doing the despised task, the thread an invisible tie to home.

Beth stabbed the needle into the block and lowered it to her lap. At least Joe slept soundly, despite the faint heat of fever chapping his lips. She rose to apply more salve to relieve the dryness and wondered if she should check on the other man. He'd been dragged there by Rebs late in the day, his complexion wan, lips a pale slash against even paler skin. A crease running along the side of his cheek and skull had left him addled. His condition appeared worsened by the filth of his uniform, the hollows of his cheeks, and the bites from the bugs that seemed to plague every one of the Rebs she'd seen.

She'd spent the evening going through the same process with his clothes as she had with Joe's, burning everything, her grandmother using Grandpa Bumgartner's old shirts and long underwear to clothe the men, a practice that would rob Gerta of every spare set of clothing she'd saved. Beth said nothing on the matter.

Joe moved his head, his open eyes staring dully at her. His tongue darted out to lick his lips.

"I just put some—"

Too late. Joe winced and pulled a face as the bitter taste of the balm on his lips permeated his mouth.

Beth couldn't help the laugh that squeezed out. Joe's mouth opened and his lips curved, as if he wanted to smile but it required more effort than he could muster. She smoothed her fingertips over his forehead. Still too warm, but not raging. Not yet, anyway.

"How do you feel?" His chest heaved on an inhale. She placed a hand on his arm to calm him. "We're taking care of you. You're safe."

His hand worked its way up and pushed at the quilt that covered his chest. She helped him peel back the layer and saw the rash of bug bites along his upper chest and shoulders. He rubbed his palm along the red spots until she stopped the motion. "My grandmother says it is best for you not to scratch. Let me get some cornstarch." She collected the items she needed and returned, spreading out the crock of salve, the container of cornstarch, and a mug full of fresh water.

She smiled down at Joe and held out the cup of water. "Can you sit up?"

His hands were on top of the thin blanket now. He pressed them into the sides of the mattress to gain leverage, but a jolt of pain slashed his expression and drew a moan from his lips.

She splayed a hand on his chest and pressed. He relaxed back with another moan that vibrated through her. She lifted his head, able to feel his efforts as she held the cup to his lips and he drank, sipping at first, then taking long gulps that revealed the depth of his thirst.

When she lowered his head, he snatched a quick breath and gave an almost imperceptible nod. "Good."

"I'll get some more." She refilled the mug three times before he seemed satisfied. As he drank, questions begged to be asked, but he seemed so weak. Each cup of water took more of an effort for him to lift his head to drink.

He closed his eyes as she began applying cornstarch to the visible bites. Her grandmother would have no qualms about applying it to all areas, but Beth's sense of propriety could allow her to go no further with her ministrations.

She worked the powder along his neck, the bristles of his beard grating against her fingertips. His mouth worked and she waited for him to speak, but his eyes remained closed. Taking a clean cloth from the pile, she dipped it in cool water and sponged his forehead and cheeks. At least he had grown calmer, his mind more aware.

Finished, she put the lid on the salve and picked up the quilt pieces. Joe's eyes opened as she took her seat, the quilt block in her hands. His eyes were tawny, a clear hazel that held more golden brown than green. Beautiful eyes. She wondered what he looked like healthy and whole, with meat on his bones and laughter on his lips. Shallow lines ran parallel to each other along his forehead. His golden brown hair, cut close to his scalp by her grandmother, was beginning to grow back in. Confederate or not, he was a handsome man. She wondered if Jedidiah had ever held the hand of a Southern woman after she'd nursed his wounds.

Joe's lips, thick with salve, curved upward. "Pretty." Her gaze flashed to his as heat rolled upward from her neck and stained her cheeks. His eyes dipped to the quilt blocks and horror swept over her. The quilt colors. That was what he'd been referring to!

The blush burned hotter as she held up the squares for him to see and for her to hide behind. "It is a beautiful color scheme. My mother puts together some of the prettiest colors. She loves to use old scraps of clothing that mean something to her." She was babbling, trying to cover the embarrassment of thinking, even for one second, that a man might think her pretty or go so far as to give her a compliment. Surely any compliment would fade once he saw the awkwardness of her steps.

"You. You're pretty."

Her hands fell to her lap, the soft drawl of his words captivating her. She swallowed hard, searching his face. "I . . ."

"Thank you for helping me."

"I try to help where I can." She shifted beneath his gaze and forced a smile. "Where are you from?"

"Carolina. North Caro . . ." The last syllable gave out on a sigh.

"Your family?"

He angled his face away. "Ben. My brother."

Such distress weighted those words that she feared to ask him anything else. With all her being she wished she knew what had happened to his brother. She placed her hand on his arm. "You need to sleep . . ." She paused at the feel of his name on her tongue, wondering how it would sound out loud. "Joe, you need sleep."

His face contorted. "Too many memories. I dream about it. The war."

Beneath her hand, she could feel the bunching of his muscles, the agitation building in him. She touched his arm. "We'll talk later. You can tell me all about Ben. I'll write a letter home for you."

"Will you stay?"

"I'll stay," she said. Her heart twisted at the simple promise that kept her at his side, as if it should mean more than a nurse offering comfort to a wounded man.

She didn't know if it was her voice or his exhaustion, but his chest heaved upward once, twice, his eyes closed, lashes a dark lightness against the frail skin beneath his eyes. She continued to stroke his arm and saw the tension ease from his jaw and lips before his breathing became steady and even.

Leaning back in the rocking chair, she considered the man before her and his frequent mention of Ben. Joe's brother meant a great deal to him, just as Jedidiah meant so much to her. She eyed the beaten-up haversack in the corner, tempted to rifle through it for some indication of who the man in front of her was. Instead, she picked up her quilt blocks, slid the needle from its place, and continued on the seam. Only when she was finished did she spread them flat on her lap, the pattern laid out in her mind, along with the colors. A black background that fit the mood of the night. She touched the outermost triangle, a dark red, like the blood sure to be shed in the coming days, like that she had already witnessed. Gerta's challenge haunted her. She wanted so much to run and hide, to be far from what was to come, but she couldn't leave her grandmother here alone.

But she wanted to. Oh, how she wanted to.

7

Shells sang through the air, an orchestra of bass notes that rocked the house and made the floor shudder. Beth bolted upright. Breaking glass added to the commotion. Joe moaned and his eyes snapped open, filled with a resigned terror. She clasped his hand and held it as she ducked her head. She stuffed her free hand against her mouth to stifle the terrified screams that threatened. Only when things quieted did she dare raise her head. Joe lay quiet and tense, eyes shut tight, lips moving. She squeezed his hand.

His eyes popped open, a mirror for the fear that must have been spilling from hers. She scooted closer to the head of the bed and lowered her face to his side. His arm brushed against her back and settled there, his hand a solid comfort on her shoulder.

"You never get used to it. Not if you think too hard."

She didn't know if the words were meant to comfort or were just an observation. Footsteps alerted her. Gerta appeared in the wide doorway, tying on a clean apron. "You stay here. I'll see if the soldier made it through the night."

"No, Grandmama." Beth lunged to her feet and checked the woman's momentum with a hand to her arm, a protective feeling toward the older woman trumping her own fear. Another shell struck. The floor rattled beneath their feet. Beth gathered her grandmother close as dust swirled around them. Gerta remained quiet, though her fingers gripped Beth tight until the vibrations settled.

Beth glanced at Joe, his hand gripped hard on the edge of the cot, knuckles white. "Stay with Joe, I'll check on the other."

"No." Gerta sprang away from Beth's grasp. "I have to check the wound. It's easier if I go." Gerta hesitated, hand on the doorknob. "Heat water. I'll have to change the bandage on Joe's shoulder next, and we don't know what or who else we'll see before the end of this." She glanced at the window, which was still covered with a quilt.

"At least I'll be able to see you from the kitchen."

Gerta nodded and stretched up to yank the quilt down. Light spilled through the panes, slashing her grandmother's face, revealing a wistful expression etched within the wrinkles and weathered skin. "It is good to feel the sunshine, it chases back the fears." Despite the words, Gerta shuddered as if chilled by the rays of heat streaming through the glass. Beth joined her at the window, relishing the moment when her grandmother faced her and stroked Beth's hair back from her face. A gesture so like her mother would make. A longing rose in her to retreat to her room and hold the quilt blocks against her cheek. Through their delicate, even stitches, she could absorb her mother's love and concern for her.

A knock on the door behind them pushed Beth's heart into her throat. She turned, half expecting to see Confederates, begging for more food, or demanding it. She relaxed upon seeing the dark face of Jim's oldest daughter, Emma.

"Daddy sent me to you, Miz Bumgartner. Said he thought you could use the help, seeing as you gonna stay and all and the Pipers is leavin' and don't need me no more."

As her father was free, so was Emma. Gerta welcomed the woman, offering her food and reminding her: "You'll be called on to work with the Rebs while you're here."

"I'm not afraid. No use bein' so, since I'm free. They's nothing they can do to hurt me."

"Have the Pipers left already?"

"It's a mess over there. Rebs been tramping over ever' inch of the house and orchard. General Longstreet had his supper there last night and told the family they should go."

"He took over the house?"

Emma snorted. "The house, the barn. They's everywhere."

"Where are they going?" Beth asked.

"To Killiansburg Cave. Ramey done hollered out as they was leaving, begging for them to take her with them because she was so afraid to be left behind with them varmints taking hold of the house."

Ramey—Beth made the connection—the Pipers' housemaid. She would have reason to be jittery about being left behind with Graybacks, what with the rumor of them not treating slaves with kindness. "What about your pa?"

"He's stayin' at the house with Mr. Nisewander. He's a stubborn one, that man. Said he wasn't leaving his house no matter how close them Rebs is. Told Pa he could leave if'n he wanted."

Jim wouldn't leave the man no matter what, Beth knew. "We'd welcome your help. There's a wounded man—"

Another shell whizzed through the air, the sound louder, closer. An explosion rocked the ground, a grinding sound ripped through the house. Emma screamed and covered her head with her apron. The front door blew open, slammed against the wall, and quaked on its hinges. Dust and debris streamed through the air, and grit burned across Beth's cheeks as she huddled next to Emma.

Deafened by the sound, it didn't occur to Beth that the sounds of screaming weren't of another shell until she saw her grandmother rise and run toward Joe. Beth joined Gerta on the opposite side of the cot as she talked softly to the terrified man. His gaze caught hers, and she white-knuckled the edge of the cot as she lowered herself to her knees beside him. His hand fumbled for hers. Gerta stroked the man's forehead, motioning for her to say something. But words would not come. She lowered her face to their clasped hands and let the tears flow.

She heard the rustle of skirts and knew Emma must have joined them as well.

"Spooked by it all," Gerta's voice was a whisper. "Must stir his memories, poor boy."

"Spooks me and I'm not even a soldier." Emma's voice trembled.

Shame crept up Beth's spine. She dried her eyes and sat back, aware of Joe's stare. He did not release her hand, and she didn't let go either until Gerta's movement caught her eye. Her grandmother had lifted her apron against her head and when she released the white fabric it was smeared with blood.

"You're hurt," Beth said.

"The door caught me."

Beth was on her feet, ripping a piece from her apron. Beneath her hands, Gerta's skin felt papery soft, fragile. The bloody scrape was nothing more than superficial, but it offered something to focus on besides the noise and crashing around them.

Gerta patted her arm. "I'll be fine. Stop fussing."

Beth retreated a step. "The bleeding has stopped."

"Then I'll check on the other soldier like I should have done fifteen minutes ago." She studied Joe, then Beth. "Talk to him. Get his mind off what he's hearing."

Beth reached to touch Joe's arm, feeling his need. Though his eyes were closed, his breathing said he was awake and trying to staunch his fears. Joe needed to be safe. "We should move him, Grandmama."

Gerta pursed her lips and glanced over her shoulder. Emma had crept away from their huddle and was now using a broom to sweep the glass from the edges of the shattered window. "You're right. We'll take him to the cellar. The noise will be less there. Emma?"

With Emma's strong shoulder on one side and Beth's on the other, Joe sat up. She could feel the bones beneath her hands, and the heat from his body radiated. If his fever became worse, she might lose him. His body could not take much more abuse in its weakened state. His knees buckled after a few steps. Beth slipped her arm around his waist, meeting Emma's arm as she did the same. The extra support steadied him as they inched along toward the door and outside.

"Take it slow, now," Emma said.

His legs, Beth saw, matched the emaciation of the rest of his body and she doubted the man capable of more than a few steps.

"Be careful of that wound," Gerta said. "I didn't patch him up for you all to drop him and have him bleeding again."

"Maybe," Emma grunted, "we shoulda rolled him in a blanket and—"

Heat curled around them, the sun hot and forceful adding to the discomfort of working so closely with the feverish man. Beth's arms were tingling from the burden as they stumped down the step from the porch, stopped to gain their breath, and gave Joe a chance to rest. His eyes were half-closed, sweat dripping down his face, which was red with the exertion.

"Joe?"

She could see him swallow, felt him try to take his own weight, but he was too weak and the effort too much.

"We best get him down there before we lose him." Emma redistributed his weight, and they moved forward. The cellar steps provided the biggest challenge. Gerta appeared with a long board that she placed over the stairs, and they laid Joe down, bracketing him on both sides and letting his weight and gravity pull him downward.

Gerta made a corner for him with blankets, and they pulled the half-conscious man to the pallet. She left to check on the other man, bidding Beth to remove the old bandage.

With gentle motions Beth unwound the strips. Joe stared, unseeing, still. She opened her mouth to speak, but the words wouldn't come. By the time Gerta returned, Joe's eyes had sagged closed and the wound was revealed.

"Emma, if you'll bring me some water and soap," Gerta said, removing her soiled apron, "I'll clean him up again. Beth, a clean apron and another light would help."

As Beth and Emma rose from the cellar into the smoggy heat, acrid with the scent of powder, Beth dabbed the perspiration from her face and rested on the top step. She stretched her leg in front of her, rubbing at the thigh and the knee, flexing her foot and relaxing it. Emma hurried by her. "You rest, Miss Bumgartner, I can fetch that apron and a lantern as easy as you."

Another shell screamed through the air, farther away, the crash causing Beth to cringe, her heart to plummet. It wasn't supposed to be like this. She had left her parents' home to fetch her new dream, not to be cornered by Lee's army like a rat in the corncrib. Across the Pipers' field she could see the mountains, and the haze that lay like the fog that had burned away early in the morning. This mist was a harbinger of destruction. A threat that already held the little town in its clutches, and the residents were the innocent victims.

"A wagon's coming. Gonna be full of wounded, you watch and see if I'm not right."

Within an hour Gerta's front parlor held five men. The low moans were harsh against Beth's ears. Emma moved with quiet efficiency among the men, offering water to those able to drink. Beth knelt at the side of one soldier, his head bandaged with cornhusks still retaining their green coloring. With cold fingers, she dared to lift away the husk, and her stomach knotted at the gore.

"He won't make it," Emma whispered against her ear. Yet the phrase took on a life of its own, roaring in her ears and mixing with the smell of blood and summer heat, unwashed bodies and . . . Beth pulled air into her lungs, and Emma's palm rubbed the area between her shoulder blades. "Done nursed a sight of things in my life. You want, I can work on this."

She raised her face to the woman, her tongue poised to deny the weakness she felt. "I—"

Emma took her arm and eased her onto a chair, fanning her face with an apron already smeared with blood.

Emma rushed down the steps of the cellar clutching a basket of old clothes. Beth didn't want to talk, she only wanted to finish ripping the linens and petticoats into strips and ignore the sounds and dust and fear gnawing at her backbone. She had to be strong.

Emma sat beside her. "North road is full of 'em." The tremor in Emma's voice could not be masked.

"I know. They're everywhere."

It was the reason Beth had sought the cellar and Joe's still form. He grew restless during the worst of it, but stilled when she spoke to him. The parlor now held ten men, toe to head in the cramped space. A surgeon had arrived hours before, working over them, oblivious to the blood smeared on his clothes or running onto the floor. Beth wished it would all go away. The men. The sound of their moaning.

"That boy about killed me," Emma said. "Sad to see the young ones who suffer."

The youngest, looking not more than fourteen, had been one of the first brought in, his frantic screeches vacillated between calling for his mother and writhing in pain from the hole in his abdomen. Beth shuddered at the memory and forced herself to pick up a petticoat. She began ripping the cloth into strips. Bandages to stop the blood of those men yet to come.

"Your grandmother works like she's young."

Beth nodded. "She's strong."

"Stronger than me."

Beth's gaze darted to the woman's face. Emma seemed strong. She was a big woman, beautiful and hard-working. "I guess that makes two of us. I wanted so badly for Grandmama to leave, but she was adamant about staying, and I couldn't leave her alone. Now," the shame of the words she was about to speak reduced her voice to a whisper, "now I wish I had."

"We'll ask the good Lord to be here with us."

Beth could only wonder how many times others had asked the same thing and now lay dying in the field, their blood staining the soil beneath them. She stood, the scraps falling to the ground, the petticoat gripped in her hand. No matter where she went, she could not escape God's failure. Her failure to save Leo. But as the ground swelled with another nearby hit from a shell, and the urge to run burgeoned inside her, she realized there was nowhere she could hide. Emma's voice lifted in fervent pleas to her God.

8

Beth leaned forward to raise the wick of the lamp. Shadows rolled back from Joe's cheeks, showing the haze of a beard. She wondered if he wore a beard normally or kept his jaw and cheeks clean shaven. Pressing the back of her hand against his cheek, the heat seared her cool palm. Was it her imagination? Her heart raced. Surely he would not die. She went down on her knees, the cold of the earthen floor permeating her skirts, and released the stopper on her anxieties.

Lifting Joe's hand, she uncurled his fingers and pressed her palm flat against his. If she closed her eyes, she could still see Leo's flushed face in the moments before the boy died. She could hear his rapid wheezes, see the skin falling away, charred, and feel the heat radiating from his little body.

For all she had done, the prayers she had prayed, still he had died in the inferno that had trapped her as well. She ghosted through the days of her recovery, unable to do anything but the most menial tasks, afraid to look at her leg and ankle and see the truth that shadowed the doctor's eyes, then her mother's and father's. And the cycle had begun again. The endless prayers for mercy, the fear of never being able to walk again.

Beth stuffed her fist against her lips, pressing, pushing back the wall of emotion that threatened to crush her. The sight of Emma's sleeping form stretched out beside her helped Beth gain control.

A soft flutter against her fingers pulled her attention down. Joe's fingers touched hers like the fragile beat of a baby bird's wings. His eyes remained closed, but his breathing had changed, grown shallower.

"Joe?"

His eyes slitted open. "Can't feel . . ."

She pressed a finger into the palm of his hand and his fingers curled inward, wrapping around her finger like a newborn.

"Can't feel what?"

"Arm."

The wound on his right side was high up on the shoulder. She stretched across him, touching his upper arm.

His nod brushed whiskers against the blanket, making a scratching sound. "It hurts."

She skimmed her hand down the length of his arm. "Your arm or the pressure?"

"Like needles."

"Can you move it?"

He tried. She could feel the muscles flex, but with a kitten's strength. His eyes opened fully, canvassing the interior. "What is this?"

"We moved you to the cellar. You were having nightmares or memories."

"Another battle."

The words rang hollow, awakening Beth's inner turmoil. "Yes. Close. Very close."

"And you're my refuge."

She sat back on her heels, confused by his choice of words. "My grandmother has done much more than I. She cleaned your wound and put a poultice on it to draw out infection."

"But it's you I remember."

"Me?"

"Your voice, talking to me."

"I—well, yes. I've tried to help where I can." Her throat closed. "It's all we can do."

His eyes closed and his tongue darted out over dry lips as another hit rattled the house above and sent down a geyser of dirt and dust to cloud the air. Emma moaned and sat up. The black woman scooted close, a piece of linen pressed to her mouth. Joe's cry came from low in his throat, and his fingers tightened on Beth's as she stroked his forehead, his jaw. Her heart squeezed at his helplessness.

"Am I dying?"

For an instant she hung suspended, afraid to make such an answer. The fever. His extreme thinness and the already exhausted state in which he'd arrived. The fever would further reduce his strength. She bit her lip to keep from crying, for surely he would recognize her distress and assume the worst. She'd never considered the other side of death's equation—the fear of dying. Only the side that feared being left alone.

His eyes were more focused, drilling into hers as he waited for her answer. "You are stronger. If you eat more . . . And we need to get this fever to break."

"Is there any bread? Soft bread." His tongue darted out to lick his cracked lips. "Haven't tasted soft bread in months."

"I'll get you some. A whole loaf to yourself, if you'd like." Beth rose, giving her legs a chance to recover from the cramped position. She did not want to consider why it was suddenly so important to her that he live. "More salve for your lips, water . . ."

"Come back?"

She turned at those two words, feeling both the desperation and the longing weighing on each syllable. It pulled at the vulnerable place buried deep within her heart, where she used to dream of being loved and needed. If she could not have love, she could cherish need.

"Miss Bumgartner?"

The deep rumbling voice came from the opening of the cellar doors. Jim.

"Your grandmama wanted me to bring this frame on down for that man before them Rebels claim it for one of the other men. Another wagon full of men came in. Almost full up there now."

She peered around until she saw Jim's large form, the cot stuck beneath his arm. "Yes, that would be wonderful."

When Jim was eye level with her, his dark face offered a wan smile. "Got Mr. Nisewander to agree to get out. He's coming here, gonna bunk in the cellar while I help."

"They're hitting close."

"That was what got the Mister convinced."

"The caves would be safer, even up north with his brother."

"He still ain't wanting to leave town, but I got him to see that your grandmama needed the help. He's said as long as he could see his house he'd be content." He lowered his voice. "Done had me go hide his money in the stone wall."

Beth glanced over her shoulder. Joe still watched them from the floor. "Can you get Joe settled?"

"Done got another cot to bring down, then the Mister. Me and Emma will set things straight while you fetch what you gotta."

Joe could hear no more than the deep rumblings of the black man and Beth's murmured responses. He could see the woman quickly glance in his direction. Saw her say something more, then turn to leave. His spirits sagged. He didn't want to be alone. Loneliness nipped at him, hollow and cold. Ben should be here, but, no, Ben was gone. Shot. He squeezed his eyes shut to try and remember the dream, or was it a vision? Every fiber of his being stretched to bring into focus the wayward images that danced along the periphery of his mind but never quite came into focus. He was hot, perhaps the images were nothing more than the result of his fever, of the wound in his shoulder.

And then there was his arm . . . tingly, numb. He couldn't feel it, but it hurt to move it. Even bunching his muscles sent out pulses of pain. A surgeon would amputate it. He'd seen it done hundreds of times, had heard the agonized screams of the men when medical supplies were low and chloroform in short supply. Arms, legs, hands, feet, it mattered not the part or pain, and all for the sake of saving the soldier's life. Joe shuddered and turned his face to the side. He tried again to make a fist and though his fingers curled some, he couldn't get them to tighten into a fist. It was all the Yankees' fault. The war. The blackness of war coated his soul.

What good would he be back home? His arm would render him useless. He would be alone and lonely. Sue, she would be there, wouldn't she? It was so hard to think, to remember . . .

The black man cast a shadow over him, and Joe turned with a gasp.

"It's time. I'll lift you to the mattress."

"I can walk."

The black man moved aside as Joe did his best to scoot into a sitting position, cursing the weakness and the heat that seemed to suck strength from him. He sat for a few seconds to steady his world, then swung his legs around. A groan slipped from his lips and the blood drained from his head. His shoulder began a steady thrum of pain. His legs burned. He felt himself slipping away, when strong arms lifted him and the icy chill of the cellar cut through the warmth generated by the cocoon of blanket left behind.

Cradled in the black man's arms, Joe could do nothing more than grit his teeth at the pain of his injured shoulder grinding against the man's chest. Once he was lying down again, the man stood over him.

"You the one who helped my people."

Joe heard the man's words through the haze. But the statement didn't make sense. Nothing did, and he knew, as hard as he tried to fight against it, that he was slipping away again. Weakness was winning, and fresh fear that he wouldn't wake up again clutched at him.

9

He's weak," Jim said, as he settled a chair next to Joe's cot.

"The fever is taking him." Beth withdrew her hand, disappointed to find Joe hotter than he was an hour previous.

She felt Jim's presence at her back. "Weak as a newborn chick."

"He needs to eat."

"They'll be time for that. The good Lord will watch over him."

Beth tensed, gaped up at the black man. "Why him and not all the others?"

Jim stared down at his feet. "The Lord giveth and the Lord taketh away . . ."

How many times had she heard that? It droned through her head like the hail of minié balls being sprayed right outside the door. It didn't make sense. None of it. "He's your enemy."

"Not mine. He's the one that came in with those slaves. They brought him in 'cause he saved their lives. Risked everything for that."

She recalled Gerta telling her of the night Joe was delivered to them. The story of three black people, but . . . "How did you know?"

Jim's eyes widened. "Done said enough."

"Jim?"

But the man was headed up the steps, probably in search of Mr. Nisewander, and she didn't press the issue. That Joe had risked his life for slaves . . . and him a Reb. But if Jim said as much, if he'd had contact with the blacks who brought Joe to Gerta, then what he said would be the truth.

As for the other, the unanswered question . . . She sat down and dug her fingers into her eyes to relieve her tension from the pounding of activity outside. Shouts, screams, the constant monotony of shells as dusk fell, as if both sides vowed to sling the last shell.

Gerta appeared in a swirl of warm air and the smell of rain. The skin around her mouth was gray, her lips pale. Beth watched as her grandmother asked Emma to take her place. The black woman's nod was reluctant, but she left. Beth rose to help Gerta into the opposite chair, beads of wetness caught in the silver strands of her hair and damp spots along her shoulders evidence of the rainfall. Gerta said nothing but pillowed her head on her arms and was asleep in seconds.

Beth tucked the loaf of bread and vegetables she'd brought for Joe beneath the cot and took up her sewing, settling in to the relative quiet, nerves drawn taut. Still, she would never be able to sleep. She dared to wander outside, filling her lungs with air riddled with smoke and the sharp odor of powder.

The air burned her eyes and spilled tears down her face. She blinked to relieve the sting. There was nothing new to be seen. No men in blue nearby to ease the worries filling her head. She retreated back down the steps to the safe huddle of humanity in the corner. Joe. Gerta. Drawing the chair closer to the light of the lamp, Beth spread salve on the rough ridges along Joe's lips. She would have had him eat the carrots and cucumbers and bread with a spread of last year's apple butter.

Now it would have to sit until the next time he awoke. At least he slept soundly.

The relative quiet only lasted until Jim appeared, Mr. Nisewander at his side, mumbling as he had always done. She just hoped the crotchety man didn't worry and fuss away Joe's strength in his times of wakefulness, or peg him for the enemy and spew the bitterness that had lived in his heart since the death of his only son at Bull Run.

"Not staying here," the old man protested. "Who's he?"

Before Jim could answer, Mr. Nisewander, spry in spite of his advanced years, darted away and pounded back up the steps into the night.

Jim gave a shrug and followed.

She reached for the quilt blocks, needing to be lost in something that reminded her of better times. Before Leo's death. After her ankle had healed, she'd done her best to help out, to play the part of the dutiful daughter, yet she'd caught her parents' shared looks of distress. Only with the passing of time and the witnessing of several of these exchanges did she realize their distress was over her.

Her fingers traced the outline of the maroon triangle against the black background in the quilt block. The next triangle was lighter in color, more red than black, the next one more orange, and the final one, yellow-orange, with the square in the middle a beautiful golden yellow. She pulled the thread taut and felt the symbolism of the colors pointing to something bright. *Hope?* she wondered bitterly. She'd had hope once. Love. Peace.

Worries crowded in. How much more could her grand-mother take? Emma? She would not allow herself to be stuffed into the cellar with Joe tomorrow but would venture out to the parlor and help as best she could. She chided herself for allowing herself to be pampered and petted. She wanted to be a nurse, and yet she had cowered in the face of duty. She would invite Emma to help her coax her grandmother to trade places with her. Gerta could care for Joe while she and Emma worked among the wounded.

Beth plunged the needle into the fabric again, forcing herself to focus on the menial task. Gerta always said there was no use borrowing trouble. They could only work with what they had, nothing more, nothing less.

A grim smile pulled at her lips as she wondered if her friend Teresa Kretzer had taken down the Union flag she had so proudly spread across the narrow main street of Sharpsburg for every Reb to see. Worry ate away the smile as an image of the flag being destroyed, the family held prisoner for the deed, bloomed in her mind. Her grip tightened on the material. The shimmer of light flickered and guttered. She smoothed the blocks on her lap. Three were joined together now. Each block's web of triangles pointing to that center square of bright hope.

A message to her from her mother. The darkness would fade as we journeyed toward the light. She knew what light her mother referred to. It was a promise she had once believed.

She moved her hand over her progress, a lump of longing rising in her heart. Her stitches would never be as small and perfect as her mother's, but they would do.

Beth leaned forward to blow out the guttering flame, hesitant to leave them in pitch blackness. Placing the blocks beside Joe, she picked up the lamp. "I'll be back," she whispered to the unconscious man.

A vise of panic squeezed Joe's insides. He couldn't see. Blackness engulfed him. Ben was there. Moving beside him through the open field, gun at the ready. Flames belched from the rifles in front of them and men on either side of him fell to the ground. He glanced to the side. Ben still ran with him, keeping pace, his face a mask of pain and resignation. He knew that face so well.

Another flash of light. Brighter. His body was shoved by an invisible force, and his gun fell from frozen fingers seconds before he fell, gasping in great mouthfuls of the green grasses. He wanted so badly to see his brother's face again . . .

"Ben! Ben!"

A hand pushed at his chest. "Joe."

It was the voice of the woman. He blinked and a whimper quaked from his throat. "He's dead."

"Shh . . ."

"He's gone."

"Drink this."

He didn't want to drink. Or eat. He wanted to escape to a place where Ben would be alive again.

"Joe. I need you to drink this. Please?"

He turned his head, stared into those clear hazel eyes and the tentacles of the dream released him with every breath. Ben was gone. He could not go where his brother was. He squeezed his eyes shut.

She touched his hair. "You've had a dream, but you're awake now."

"You know me." He closed his mouth over the dryness, worked his jaws. "I don't know your name."

Her mouth curved. "Elizabeth. Beth, or Bethie if you're my mother."

There was humor there, dancing in her eyes. He drank it in, but like a man drinking too fast in order to quench his thirst, his stomach rebelled. Reality slapped back at the brief levity. "Did you see him?"

"Your brother?"

He nodded and lifted his hand to cover his mouth as another groan escaped. Tears scorched his throat. The dreams had brought it back. Pieces that he could fit together enough to guess the truth. He'd fallen to the ground. Shot. The Yankees . . . Ben had slammed him down flat and dragged him to a barn.

Her hand touched the back of his hand, turned it, and grasped it between hers. "I am so sorry."

"He didn't bring me here."

She hesitated. Shook her head. "No."

"Then how . . . ?"

"I was asleep." She shifted but tightened her grip on his hand. A warm hand. Soft. "My grandmother heard something, I guess. She found three blacks, you were with them. They wanted her to care for you. Said you were shot, but that you'd saved their lives." Her smile flattened. "I don't know details."

Ben wasn't with them, and he knew his brother was dead. The focused answer of how, when, and where eluded him. He'd dreamed something about Ben, but it, too, slipped the grasp of his mind.

"You should eat something." Her hand lay flat against his forehead, smooth and cool. The dark room beyond the circle of light revealed nothing of where he was. He felt strange. She was his only connection to life. As if it were only the two of them wrapped in a world of frozen dreams.

She didn't wait for an answer, instead uncovering a basket of bread and a jar of apple butter. As he watched her rip off a piece and spread it with the glorious sweetness, his appetite stirred and grew into a raging beast. Only manners, coated with a heavy dust of disuse, kept him from picking up the remainder of the loaf and biting into it like a starving animal. He accepted the morsel she handed him, forced himself to take measured bites, savored the sweetness on his tongue.

He drank the water she handed him, feeling the stream of cool liquid slide down his throat and fill his empty stomach. Cucumber slices and carrots tempted his tongue, but he filled up on the bread, taking only nibbles of the vegetables.

Her fingers stroked his forehead, and he couldn't help wondering if he looked as terrible as he felt. "Beth," he whispered.

She paused, her gaze catching his in the flickering light of the lantern. "You're still warm."

He raised his hand, touched the soft part of her upper arm. "What is happening?"

Her eyes flared with an emotion he could not define, then the tautness of her expression cleared. "You mean the war?"

"I—" It stuck in his throat. War. The sounds of his dreams, the running and belches of fire. He'd been a soldier. He stared down the length of himself, but the blanket held its secrets. His right hand seemed weak, hard to move, and pain pulsed through his chest from his right shoulder. None of it made sense, but the pieces were all there. Waiting for him to put them all together.

10

Joe watched the woman pick up a piece of dark material and fold it together with another piece. All traces of mirth were gone. He saw fatigue in the planes of her face, the shadows of her eyes, and the slow, methodical motions she used to fold the material she held. The deeper part of him wanted to demand that she give him every bit of information she could, but looking into her eyes, his need melted away. She had already shared what she knew. By the creaks from the floor above their head and the rumbling of voices and the unmistakable moans of the wounded, it was clear that the war rambled on, leaving broken bodies in its wake.

"My grandmother might be able to tell you more about those who brought you here." Her face lit and she snapped her fingers. "Your satchel!" He gave her his full attention as she stood and rushed into the darkness beyond the reach of light. In her absence, the darkness pressed closer. He wanted to follow her and cursed his weakness. Just as he thought he might try to sit up, she returned and set a dirt-caked bag beside him. His haversack. He recognized the ragged strap, and another memory nudged at him. Ben throwing it to him after they bivouacked for the night. The haversack's light weight slapping against his shoulder. Only his most prized possessions within it. He'd seen men cast theirs aside over time when in the heat of battle, but he kept his close. The little book of poetry. A Bible. A picture of Sue in her wedding dress.

Ben had kept his haversack close, too, but somewhere along the march to Fredericksburg, he'd given it up, or lost it, Joe couldn't recall which. And then the battle had erupted at South Mountain and they'd been spread so thin, the Yanks nipping at their heels. He tried to hang on to the memory and force his mind to grasp more details, but they spun away. "I can't remember."

"We'll work on it together."

It was Beth who lifted the flap of his haversack. She withdrew the Bible first and handed it to him. He ran his hand over the softness of the leather cover, worn, cracked by age, lightly caressed the pages, made buttery from wear. Inside the front cover, a list of births and deaths. The first births written in his mother's flowing script, the deaths written in the same hand, the letters more loosely formed, and he knew his mother must have cried through each of those entries.

"A box."

Joe accepted the slim wooden box Beth handed him. A smile crept up his cheeks as he opened the lid, knowing exactly what lay within. "My fishing hook! Ben always teased me about this, but he stopped when we didn't have anything to eat but were able to catch fish." The memory came easy. He tugged out a "housewife," the sewing kit. Two buttons lay in the bottom. He'd never sewed them back on. Too tired. Not caring at that point. A handkerchief filled the corner next to the buttons, its initial, stitched in blue . . .

"A woman's likeness."

He held out his hand for the familiar item, his throat closing at the sight of Sue's creamy complexion and slight smile.

He absorbed her expression and felt the fist of grief slam him hard.

———⁂———

Across Joe's features marched a display of emotion. When his features pulled tight at the sight of the picture, Beth's heart sank. When Joe closed his eyes and pressed the likeness to his chest, despair washed over her. She leaned back in the chair and balled her hands in her lap, wondering why she felt such disappointment. She understood his emotions at seeing the beautiful woman. His wife, no doubt. Deep down anger bubbled up. Why did it matter? He had someone to love. All that they had shared was nothing more than the product of his need and the strain they were under. Nothing more.

She felt bereft, just as she'd felt the day they'd buried little Leo. His mother's muffled sobs had felt more like an accusation. She had tried to rescue the boy and failed. She could still hear his screams of terror as the fire raged. She'd plunged inside without thought for herself, turned back by the thick smoke, choking, unable to see Leo, confused by the roar of flames. She'd retreated until, right at the door, the beam had fallen and caught her leg. Only the quick response of a neighbor lifting the beam away had given her time to escape the collapse of the entire house.

Beth stroked the dark background of the quilt blocks, touched the darkness, and realized how it had seeped into her soul. A somber place, where comfort and joy drank from the same desultory source of fear and injustice. If there were light around her, she could not see it. Fear held her bound and gagged to the blackness.

"Sue died."

Beth angled her face, catching Joe's low words. So he had known love and loss too. She dared not explore the reason for relief and forced herself to focus on the man. And see his pinched features, and the hard way he swallowed. "I'm so sorry."

She touched the back of his hand, and his composure shattered into sobs that wrenched her heart. She pulled his hand into hers and held it firm as the tears came, streaming golden paths from the corners of his eyes to the meager pillow that held his head. Tears stung her own eyes as well as she witnessed Joe's show of emotion. She pressed the handkerchief from the box into his hand, the fragile stitching of a blue "S"— evidence of the one it had once belonged to.

She wanted so much to cradle him close and take away all the bad. If only she could touch the spot that ached within him and mold it into something fresh and full of hope. Was that how her mother and father had felt about her? She squeezed her eyes shut, releasing the tears gathered there to course down her own cheeks. One led to another, until a steady stream flowed down to drip onto her skirt.

Joe's face lay in profile to her, his sobs easing, the handkerchief put to good use. When he laid it aside, he met her gaze, searching for something she didn't understand. "You must think me a fool . . ."

A final swipe of her apron across her cheek took care of the last of her tears. "Not at all. There is so much heartache."

"It's the one thing that crosses the lines without penalty."

She inhaled, considering. "There is hope," she wanted to say, but they were her mother's words, not her own. "It's time to rest. Now, while it's quiet. Do you need anything?"

"I'll be fine."

"Would you like me to leave the picture with you?"

"No. It was a long time ago . . ." He lifted the Bible, testing its weight, then tried to use the back of his hand to open the flap of the haversack. She brushed his feeble attempts away and eased the Bible within, followed by the wooden box.

"What about you? You lost anyone in the war?"

Beth stilled. "My brother joined up."

"But he's alive?"

"As far as we know." She shifted her weight and tucked her weak leg beneath her stronger one. She had no heart for this conversation or the reminder that someone else lay at the mercy of Lee or the newly appointed McClellan.

"Sue was devastated when her husband was killed at Fort Sumter. She just lost heart after that. Mama done her best to—" He choked on the words.

She hated herself for having to ask. "Sue's husband?"

He nodded. "My sister."

His *sister*. She held up the quilt pieces, blocking her face from his view. She was encouraged by the idea that Sue had not been his wife. "My mother sewed this."

"Right pretty. My mama loved to piece and sew. Sue had herself a stack of quilts at her marriage to Laurence."

"What do you see when you look at this?" She peeked over the top.

"Look like suns. Could use us some sunshine."

She knew he wasn't referring to the weather. "There's more . . ." She lowered her arms and pointed to the center square. "See how the colors lead to the brightest spot?"

"Hope in the midst of darkness."

The way he said it held such reverent awe. "It's what I saw, too."

"Your mother knew you were going into trouble?"

"I wanted to be a nurse," her laugh was without humor. It was more than that and she knew it. "Mama worried over me because of something that happened some years back." She had his attention and wondered if she could give voice to the event that had so changed the direction of her life. His own tragic story of his sister's love and loss emboldened her, and the story of Leo slipped out with an ease underscored by the press of his good hand against hers when she stumbled over the part of the beam falling and trapping her.

She could recall again the smell of singed flesh, the unbelievable heat juxtaposed with the swell of the cool air that promised freedom from the jaws of the raging beast. She'd prepared herself to die there, never expecting the lifting of her body before she lost consciousness, every shallow gasp for air filling her lungs with the heat of the inferno.

"Reckon God was watching over you pretty good that night."

She flinched and frowned. God? Had He been watching over Leo as well? Joe didn't know about the lasting scars on her leg, thigh, and lower body. All he saw was that she was alive and whole.

"So your mama knew how guilty you felt and wanted you to know there was hope."

His statement stole air from her lungs. Was that why she was living? Hope? His statement turned over and over in her mind and she still could not make sense of it. If life was hope, then she was better off dead.

"Beth?"

Her throat seized up and she slipped her hand out from under his. She avoided the searching eyes.

"Are you leaving?"

"Sleep well."

"You, too," he turned his head, eyes capturing hers as she stood to slide the haversack beneath the cot. "Could you . . . would you read to me? Tomorrow?"

What did tomorrow hold? During the moments she had sat next to Joe, the war outside had given way to a fresh battlefield. One they shared, and yet his last words left her feeling stale and old beyond her years.

"The Confederates surround us. They're parked in the fields around us. Everywhere." Joe had no way of knowing their dire straits, though he would understand the suffering of the soldiers and their mind-set. She softened, wanting . . . something that she didn't understand. "If tomorrow allows, I will."

His eyes hazed over, a spark of anger flashing. "It's that bad?"

"It's a fearful thing." She picked up the lantern.

She emerged into the night, Mr. Nisewander's cranky voice skittering through the eerie quiet.

". . . dark cellar with creepy things. I'm staying right here."

Beth lifted the chimney and blew out the lantern. Jim sure had his hands full. She heard the black's voice, injected with a placating note. She paused in the yard and lifted her chin. Darkness blanketed the rolling hills. If the Yankees were there, there was no sign of them, but the soldiers who were brought to them talked of skirmishes, of the battle on top of South Mountain and the Yankees at their heels.

A volley of shots split the quiet of night. Beth's heart slammed against her ribs. Lifting her skirts, she hurried up the porch step and into the house, where the only light flickered from deep in the parlor filled with groaning, reaching men. With certainty she knew there would be no room for her after tomorrow. She would lose her bed, her room, her privacy. She returned to the porch. Both Jim and Mr. Nisewander had heard the shots, the older man's head cocked in such a way as to display his unrelenting attitude. Behind him, Jim just shook his head.

"Nothing more than a nervous guard with a heavy trigger finger," the old man groused before turning and tottering toward the front door. He weaved among the men littering the floor and toward the steep staircase. "I'll sleep sound as the dead."

She winced at the baldness of the statement. Jim watched the man go.

"Does Emma need help?"

"No, ma'am. Most of the soldiers are sleeping well, except the one . . ." his head tilted toward the parlor room, where the men lay. "It doesn't look like that one will be with us come morning." He paused to stretch. "If'n you don't need me, I think I'll head down to the barn for the night."

"You'd be safer in the cellar."

"Yes, ma'am. Makes even a free man worry when there's so many Graybacks around. Them," he jerked his head toward the parlor, "I've no reason to fear since they're too banged up to notice the color of my skin, but the awake ones make me worry."

"Joe won't hurt you, Jim. Not if he risked his life to save other blacks."

"Then I'll look after him as well as I do Mr. Nisewander, ma'am."

Why did that bit of kindness twist her up so much? "Thank you, Jim."

He shouldered by her. Nothing stood in the way of her sleep now except the litany of moans. With heavy heart she climbed the steps, afraid of the darkness. Even more afraid of the light.

11

September 17, 1862

The first crash of artillery broke the silence of the early dawn and agitated the wounded men. Emma's dark eyes rolled with fright as her hand butterflied the hem of her fresh apron. Both Gerta and Emma looked exhausted and Beth doubted either had slept. She knew she had done little but yank the covers up in fear or push them off when she got too hot. A miserable night. Fear permeated everything; even the air seemed laden with a sickening sour smell. Maybe it was the scent of the unclean bodies mixed with blood.

Jim appeared, wide-eyed with concern over the barrage of bullets and shells that beat the air full of holes every second. "Didn't take much to move Mister from the guest room to the cellar."

The statement would have been humorous if it hadn't so accurately defined the danger. Beth swallowed. More shells, in a deafening, consistent onslaught that vibrated the walls.

Gerta rushed inside carrying a bucket of water.

Jim darted forward. "Let me take that."

"Get these men moved to the back room, Jim. They're clean. We're going to have an epidemic on our hands if more are brought in and they're as dirty as these." Her petite form twisted to gaze over her shoulder at the writhing, moaning men before she faced Beth and Jim again. Her lips compressed into a tight, thin line. "We lost Shem in the night."

The two shared a glance and Beth understood the silent message between them. She had seen the large earthen hole from her bedroom window. Jim must have worked on the grave throughout the night, yet he showed no signs of weariness.

Jim nodded at Gerta and splashed his bucket of water into the kettle over the fire. "More water?"

"That, too," Gerta acknowledged, the high color on her cheeks giving away her level of stress.

Beth stepped into the parlor, noting the relative stillness of the men in the silver gray of dawn. Only an occasional moan punched the air. Then there was the still form in the corner, the bandage on his head bloody, the wood planking beneath him saturated in blood. Shem looked peaceful. A tremor vibrated deep down inside of Beth, a quivering that never completely left as she helped where she could throughout the morning.

Shells and gunfire exploded. Screams punched the air from both the injured brought to them and those outside. Another shell beat at their house, hitting close enough to rock the floor. Emma screamed, and the men joined her chorus, some trying to rise, others only groaning their terror. Beth covered her ears and shrank back against the wall, feeling it shudder. Smoke and dust rose in a cloud.

"Get into the cellar," Gerta yelled at her.

Beth and Emma exchanged glances, each knowing the other could not abandon the elderly woman.

Beth spoke first. "You can't do this yourself."

Gerta's blue eyes held hers. "You're not afraid?"

She was terrified, expecting any minute to be her last. But her vulnerability didn't match that of the men in their care. "I'm staying."

"Check on Jim. He's digging another hole."

There was no time to think, only to act. Another shell screamed and landed, piercing her ears until she couldn't hear her feet on the wooden planks of the porch as she hurried down the step. No time to consider the danger that being outdoors posed. The black man worked fast, muscles straining as he plunged the shovel deep into the earth, stomped it down deep with his big feet, and pulled a shovelful of the rich soil from the ground. As soon as he saw her coming, he motioned her away.

"Don't need nothing. Get on inside." He stilled, eyes flicking down the road. "'Nother wagon coming."

It meant more wounded. As the sun climbed higher in the sky, the sounds raged on. Beth kept moving, indicating places to put more men, afraid being still would awaken her to what movement muffled. A Confederate surgeon's assistant arrived and began sorting the men based on the severity of their wounds. He commandeered the dining table and set up a makeshift operating table in the open air.

A woman ran down the street, hair flying behind her, under each arm a sack leaking grain as she ran. Two little boys yanked the hand of an even smaller girl trailing behind them, her legs stretching to meet the pace, their faces showing their panic.

The urge to join them tempted Beth. She couldn't think about it or she would do it. She was needed. Jim loomed in front of her. "Get on with ya, Missy. Send Emma on out to help."

She swallowed. Dust floated through the air like a fog and settled a dry layer in her throat. She coughed and lunged for the house just as another wagon stopped. Stretcher bearers passed her en route to the house, droplets of blood marking their grim paths. She lifted her skirts to free her feet.

A maelstrom of activity greeted her. More groaning, one man screaming at the top of his lungs. Confederate men nodded to her as they passed. One planted himself right in front of her.

"Best place for you, ma'am, is far away from here." His drawl was pronounced, covering each word with warm syrup. His eyes were kind, his countenance gim.

"I live here. I want to help."

"The South?"

"Side makes no difference. They are all men needing someone."

The man stared at her with a bittersweet expression that seemed out of place. "Then we welcome your bravery and thank you for your sacrifice."

"I make it for the Union as well."

The man nodded. "I understand."

She scrambled inside in time to see Gerta dipping out more hot water. "Bandages. Anything you can find. Blankets, linens, dresses . . ."

She ran up the steps and pulled down her skirts and snapped the folds out of her best nightgowns, forcing herself not to think. Emma stopped at the doorway with an armful of men's clothes. Beth's grandfather's, probably stored in the attic.

"I'm leaving these here. There's more. She wants them ripped up too."

A shell boomed and the side of the house rocked. Emma threw the clothes into the air and immediately broke into tears.

"Make it stop. God, make it stop!"

Beth knelt in front of the woman, her own tears breaking the surface. Another hit and the window shattered, shards tinkling over the spot she'd just vacated. Smoke billowed into the room.

"Fire. There's fire!" Emma surged to her feet. Beth grabbed her hand and held it firm, but Emma yanked free and bolted out of the room.

❈

Air leached from Joe's throat as he pushed himself upright. At least the old man's ranting about Rebels and "seceshers" had died down with the last blast. The words had rained down on him most of the morning, rising in their vileness when the blasting was at its worst, lessening as the battle seemed to fade and the man's voice cracked with the strain.

He'd been quiet for too long now and Joe determined to make sure he wasn't harmed. It was semidark, the low light of the flickering candle Jim had lit unable to reach the width and depth of the cellar. Joe squinted, careful not to stare directly into the flame, but beyond it toward the last place he'd heard the sound of the man's voice. The man was there, slumped in a chair. Joe debated going to him, but his ears still burned with the hateful words against the South that mirrored his hatred for the North. But the man was still, too still.

Joe struggled to a sitting position. He'd not seen Beth all morning and he wondered, even hoped, that she had left for shelter far away from the frenetic chaos of war. He heard enough tramping around above his head to know many more occupied the house than had the previous day. The fury of the battle was only slightly muffled by the cellar. He felt trapped in the hole, afraid to be in the thick of the battle but equally afraid to flee and brand himself a coward. A continuous rattle of gunfire and screams rocked and shook the house. Pebbles of dirt and dust filled the room until his lungs felt clogged with the debris. Men moaned and screamed above him. Joe used his sleeve to wipe beads of sweat from his brow.

He squeezed his eyes shut, his chest tight with anxiety. Any minute, and the house could crash down around him. He forced his mind to other things. He inhaled slowly, feeling like his mind would splinter in a thousand different directions.

The creak of the cellar doors hailed someone's arrival. Two men, a stretcher between them, surged down the steps and laid a man on the floor. They left and returned with another. The fetid stench of unwashed bodies permeated the air. The old man remained miraculously quiet.

Three men in total were delivered to the cellar, and on the heels of the stretcher bearers' exit, Beth, a black woman at her side, came down the cellar steps. She appeared to be cradling the black woman, whose cries were audible, if not hysterical.

Joe lay his head down and swallowed, lips working. It had been a long time since he'd uttered a prayer. There was blackness in his soul. He knew it. After Sue died, there had been no merciful God. His mother's death, his father's mental decline, the destruction of all he'd known by the Union had congealed, then hardened into hatred. He had never understood God's hand in taking Sue, but he'd seen enough death and suffering since joining the Army of Northern Virginia to know God was Someone to whom a dying man must make his peace. His mother had pressed the Bible into his hands, as a memory of home and a symbol of her faith. Her death had been the propulsion for him and Ben to join the army and spend the rage they harbored against the enemy.

And now Ben was gone, too.

He tried to remember home and wrap himself in the anger he'd felt before joining, but there was no anger left. He swung his legs to the floor and pulled himself up, gritting his teeth against the pain and numbness of his shoulder. The numbness scared him the most. It marked him as useless. Shells rattled in a constant barrage now. The boom of cannons gave him strength as he lunged for his haversack. His shoulder muscles contracted tight and hard. His weakened limbs almost gave way as he tried to straighten. He panted from exhaustion and dragged the haversack to within arm's reach of the cot. His knees gave way and he slammed onto the thin mattress. The jolt thrust fresh pain through his body and beaded sweat on his forehead, which trickled down into his eyebrows and burned his cracked lips.

He rested, heart slamming with the exertion and fear. More dust lifted to obscure his vision and choke him as the cannonading became a constant roar. The men writhed on the floor, calling for someone to care for them. For help he could not give. With shaking hand, he lifted the flap of the haversack. He'd been writing a letter, he remembered, to . . . A hot hand squeezed him and his head throbbed. He lay back and wept, disgusted with his weakness, his inability to move, the uselessness of his right arm, and the dark, cold fear.

He felt the presence of her before he felt her touch and heard her voice. The constant noise of the battle had waned. Dust still filled the air, making Beth seem a hazy presence. But he welcomed it.

"How are you doing?"

He blinked at the brightness of the lamp she carried.

"Sorry."

The light receded a bit, and he turned to face her. She sat there as if every drop of energy had drained from her body and puddled on the floor and she had no way to claim it again. Yet she was here. She had stayed to help. *He* wanted to help. To ease the burden hunching her shoulders.

"Beth?"

She raised her eyes to his, her gaze clinging, tears pooled on her lower lashes. Another shell rocked the house and she was up, running toward the steps before he could say anything.

His nerves were drawn tight by the whimpers from the men around him. He was shattering and he knew it. Struggling up onto his elbow, his right arm almost numb, his shoulder protesting the movement, he sat on the edge of the bed again, willing strength into his legs and body. He smashed his fist into the mattress and eased himself to his bare feet, the cold earthen floor barely registering. His world spun. He reached out to the wall, his legs shaking with the effort. He needed to check on the others. See if he knew them. They were on his side. And the old man, too, needed someone.

Joe's legs quaked. He fought for equilibrium before he slid to his knees. A gasp slipped out at the impact. Pain pushed blackness into his vision and his consciousness shrank to a pinprick.

12

Gerta protested all the way down the cellar steps. "It's nothing more than a scratch."

"You're bleeding," Beth said, countering the woman's persistence, thankful that the shelling had stopped, allowing them respite.

"And I feel fine."

"You're exhausted."

"Everyone is."

"Then use this time to rest. The surgeon seems to have everything well in hand."

Gerta snorted, the most unladylike response Beth had ever heard from her grandmother. "I'll rest, but there will be more. It's not over."

There was nothing more to say. Her grandmother would die trying rather than curl up in a corner. And Beth had good reason to fear. Gerta's color wasn't good, her breathing seemed more labored than usual.

"Where's Emma?" Gerta asked.

"She's down here." Another worry. The black woman seemed on the verge of hysteria. "I sent Jim down to be with her."

"Good, I didn't like the way that fancy captain was eyeing them."

Beth helped her grandmother down that last step, and Gerta rushed forward and knelt at the side of one of the new arrivals who had yet to be given attention. Beth pushed back a sigh. No matter how much she harped or expressed concern, her grandmother's heart was set on helping. She turned her head and saw Jim in the corner, lifting a limp form in his arms.

Joe.

"Found him like this," Jim murmured as she came to the big man's side. "Came to get the lantern, and there he was."

Beth heard something else in Jim's voice. "Emma?" she whispered.

"Told her to go to Killiansburg Cave. There's a steady stream of people on the road, running for all they worth." He turned his face away. "She took Mr. Nisewander."

"He didn't put up a fight?"

"No fight left in him. He could hardly talk. Like his mind had left him. Emma led him away like a sheep."

"You should have gone, too."

He nodded. "Should have. Probably wish I had before too long, but I couldn't leave seein' as Miz Gerta needs me."

Beth checked the bandage on Joe's shoulder, grateful to see it remained clean. She turned, digging in the deep pocket of her apron for another roll of bandages and knelt beside Gerta, biting back a weary sigh.

"Water?" Jim spoke the single word as a question.

"And the surgeon," Gerta responded. "Be my best guess he'll want to take this leg off."

Beth turned her face away at the mangled mess of the limb. She'd seen so much more in the last few days than she'd ever experienced before. Gerta moved on to the man next to him. She put out a hand to help her descent and slipped in a dark puddle. Her hand came up bloody, and she rubbed it down her blood-stained apron. Beth's eyes went over the man, trying to assess the wound, seeing nothing wrong with the man's torso, or his arms or face. She looked at her grandmother, Gerta's steady gaze meeting hers.

"He's gone."

"But . . . ?"

Gerta rose, the lower part of her skirt soaked with blood, and it came to Beth in slow degrees what her grandmother didn't bother to explain. The blood said it all. He'd been shot in the back, perhaps in his head.

Jim came down the steps and placed a pail of water on the floor inside the opening to the cellar, then retraced his steps.

Beth sucked air into her lungs, having no choice but to move on to the next man to keep up with her grandmother. The man moaned low in his throat and writhed from side to side, the hole in his abdomen saying more than words. Gerta shook her head. He would not last long.

They went over to the last two men, neither conscious, the earth below them drinking in their life's blood. Gerta straightened. "They must have brought the worst ones down here."

Beth retreated to the corner beside Joe's cot. She pressed her back to the wall, the coolness seeping through her thin dress, welcome but chilling. Of the five men in front of her, one was dead and the other four were dying, unconscious except for the ever-diminishing moans of the gut-shot man as he bled out onto the floor.

Exhaustion weighted her head and she cradled it on her arms, blanking her mind. Within minutes she'd drifted but was jerked back to reality by the hard vibration of shelling. Gerta sat in the chair, arms folded against the cot. She had heard the last shell, too. Another one came, this one farther away.

"Oh, God, have mercy." Gerta said, her voice soft. She made as if to stand and a new anxiey drummed fear into Beth's veins.

"Grandmother, please rest. They can handle things for a while."

If not persuaded by Beth's words, Gerta's hand to her head must have been the convincing factor. Without asking, Beth withdrew a bandage she'd never used from her apron and wiped the blood congealed on Gerta's temple with one corner. Already it had caked in her grandmother's hair. She crossed and dipped her apron into the water, wrung it, and returned to dab at the blood. With deft fingers she put a strip around Gerta's head, then another. Her grandmother's fingers rose to still her actions.

"Save the rest for another."

Supplies were low. Even the surgeon's assistant had admitted it.

Beth ripped the linen, pulled back her grandmother's mussed gray hair, and tied it with the cloth strip to keep the bandage in place.

"Beth."

She turned toward the rasping whisper. Joe's dull gaze was on her and her hand went to his forehead. "I'm here." She saved the most obvious question.

Joe's hand rose, fingers splayed. An invitation.

She tucked her hand into his, reassured by the warmth and bond they'd forged. Gerta had been correct. It didn't matter that he was a Confederate. It only mattered that he was here, now, and needed her help.

"I want to walk."

Gunfire sounded, close, glass shattered, streams of dirt and dust snaked down the walls. She eyed the support beam, praying it would hold. Joe was shoving his way upright. She could see the weakness; the uselessness of his right arm was more than apparent as she shouldered under it to aid his rising. He wobbled, shifted his weight onto her to the point that she felt her legs protest. And then he jerked downward again, hitting the mattress harder than he'd meant to. His moan added to the misery of the dust. Jim appeared alongside.

"He wants to walk. Then I'll do the lifting."

The big black man stood next to Joe, his weight twofold that of the underfed soldier. They walked a few steps before Joe gasped to be let down again. It was Gerta who handed the man a carrot and a jar of preserves, and bid him to eat.

"You'll mend. Your body needs nourishing."

"Why did you get up on your own? You knew you were weak." Beth frowned at him.

"The old man. He was quiet. Too quiet. I thought he'd . . ."

"Won't bother you none now," Jim said as he lowered himself, cross-legged, to the dirt floor. "He left with my daughter."

The soldier's moans were quieter. Joe's eyes took in the spectacle of the wounded. "What about them?"

Gerta shook her head.

Beth shared a look with Joe before he turned his head away, his jaw working.

They huddled close to Joe's cot as he ate with slow movements. He said little, and there was little to say. Gerta cradled her head on her arms and slept. Beth's tension eased at her grandmother's surrender to sleep. Even a few hours would prove a great benefit to the woman. At some point during the renewed shudder of cannonading and gunfire, screams and yells, Beth found her hand again cradled in Joe's. She couldn't remember which one of them had initiated the touch, and it did not matter. It grounded her. Injected comfort while the world outside the cellar tumbled and rocked.

"Tell me about your home."

Beth flinched. "Home?"

Joe's tongue flicked across his lips, and he nodded. "Do you live with your grandmother?"

"I do now." Her throat closed over the words.

"Why did you leave home?"

She laughed, a humorless sound. "I wanted to be a nurse."

Joe's smile was fleeting, incongruous. Tasting the irony of what she said in light of the reality of the situation. "And your parents didn't want you to?"

She considered the question. "They'd just lost Jedidiah to the war. I guess they worried they might lose me, too." She understood that fear now, in the midst of such a fierce, confusing battle, where the dying gasps of the soldier punctuated every new blast.

"That's why she gave you the quilt. So you could see beyond the hard times."

"Are you a preacher?"

Joe shook his head. "No. Just seems like something a mother would think of."

It was true. The quilt was her mother's quiet way of reminding her of this truth, and the best gift her mother could give.

"My mother sewed all kinds of things," Joe offered, his voice resigned, heavy with tension and dread.

The question perched on her tongue to be asked, but she swallowed it back, afraid to hear that his mother had been killed. It wouldn't be fair that he had lost both sister and mother.

"Tell me about Sue."

This time the smile lit his eyes. "My twin. She was always in trouble." His lips clamped together and he turned his head away. "She'd just been married."

Another crash quaked the ground. She caught her breath and held it as she huddled over Joe's cot. She straightened and tried to keep the words flowing. "My mother and father own a farm north of here."

"Brothers? Sisters?"

"Two brothers. Jedidiah, I told you about. Thomas is married, much older than us because my mother lost children between his birth and Jedidiah's."

"That must be the worst, losing a child. My mother never quite recovered after Sue . . . It made Ben more determined to join the South and I—"

She watched his profile, his jaw working. His hand squeezed hers a little harder, an action she was sure he was not conscious of.

He stared ahead, eyes narrowed. "I followed him to keep him out of trouble."

"You're remembering things. That's good."

His brow knit. "Bits and pieces." He released her hand and massaged his eyes, his chest shuddering as he inhaled. Shells hit in quick succession. Beth leaned toward her grandmother. Jim scooted along the ground, closer to them, as if his presence could protect them from harm. Joe's fingers interlaced with hers and she pressed her forehead against their clasped hands, fighting tears. A scream rose in her throat. *Not again! God, not again!* Terror clawed as the dirt began tumbling down the walls, dust rising in a weak cloud that coated her mouth.

Joe's hand cupped her cheek. The show of sympathy released her emotions, and sobs crawled up her throat. She lowered her face to her arms to muffle the sound. Joe stroked her hair, her arm, then clasped her hand again in a grip that revealed his level of distress.

The sound of the raging battle ebbed and flowed as the afternoon stretched into evening. Like prisoners they huddled, captured by the war outside and the death rattle of the dying soldier. And when quiet finally stilled the night, the breathing of the injured soldier on the floor stilled as well.

13

No one tried to stop Beth as she crawled from the cellar. She had to see for herself. Bullets still split the air, but the action came from the direction of Harper's Ferry at the west end of town. She felt suffocated in the cellar. Afraid. The sudden need to see for herself rose up, growing so strong that she could no longer see the insanity of venturing out.

Smoke curled in a thick cloud to the west, against the red sunset. The same red as the triangles in the quilt. Shells screamed, farther away, almost drowned out by the moans and screams that pummeled from every direction. Men lay in the yard of her grandmother's house now. An able-bodied assistant she'd seen earlier came from the springhouse bearing a yoke of water pails. At some point, a fire had been started, the snap of the blaze and the heat added to the misery of the men sprawled nearby. Her stomach clenched as her gaze collided with the spectacle of the surgeon's table, a pile of amputated appendages drawing flies. Bile coated her throat and mouth, and she staggered, oblivious to the moaning and the clutching hands that reached for her as she passed. A groan rose in her throat. It was too much. Her town. The men. Rebels who had come to destroy, and yet they had been destroyed, one by one.

She rushed up the road as fast as her throbbing ankle would allow. Confederates clogged the road. Wagons, horses pulling cannons. She turned and went east, where the stain of darkness limned the horizon.

Her heart slammed pain into her chest. She stopped, a hand to her throat, seeing nothing familiar about the town, though in another way everything was familiar. Teresa's flag was gone, and she wondered if it had survived, if Teresa and her family had left or stayed, were dead or alive.

Heat from the blazes stroked her cheeks, some fresh and just getting started, others, starved for fuel, dwindled and smoked. A choking haze laced her every inhalation. At the crest of the east end of Main Street she saw the worst and halted in abject horror. A dark shape shifted to block her view.

"Go back, ma'am. You should have left with the rest of them."

"You've killed us," she whispered, her voice ragged and hoarse. "All of them . . ."

"Get back, I tell you."

A wagon creaked up beside her. "Elizabeth Bumgartner?"

"I've ordered her away," the soldier stated flatly to the man. "If you can take her on . . ." He walked away, a stripe down his hazel trousers and linen shirt showing his rank. He was used to being obeyed.

The man on the wagon was beside her. "I thought you'd be with your parents. Come with me and I'll take you back."

The words were a hailstorm. She tried to collect the loose threads of her thoughts, staring again at the field in front of her, the cannons to her right and left. The milling about of soldiers, the shouts. All Rebels. Ragged, dirty Rebels. And in front of her, nearly at her feet, bodies. Blood, moans, screams.

"Come with me, Elizabeth."

The name jolted her, and she pulled against the man's hand, tilting her head to see his face. She knew him. He knew her. And despite the shock of what she'd seen, she recognized the face of Riley Mercer. The soft edge of a boy's jaw now hardened by maturity. Riley had loved her once. Before Leo and the injury . . .

"Yes." The word sounded wooden and dead, like she felt.

He said not a word as he helped her into the wagon. Erect, she could see into the bed, the tangle of limbs, heard the same low moans of pain. Blood. Her knees gave out and she sat, staring straight ahead, this view not much different.

Riley was talking. She tried to focus on his words. Closed her eyes and wished she could close her ears to the roar of the fires and the distress of injured men, screams and gunfire and . . .

". . . school days. Never prepared us for such as this."

"No."

She hadn't heard anything about Riley since returning to Sharpsburg. Why was he here and not with his wife in Mercersville, where he belonged?

"Where's your wife?"

He stopped talking and she didn't care how harsh the words sounded. Lina had been her best friend. Before the injury. They'd talked of Riley's desire to court her, and his shyness.

"She's home with the children."

"Children." This time the bitterness saturated her word.

He took up the reins, and the wagon lurched forward. "Where would you like to go?"

As if they were out for a Sunday picnic. She pressed her lips together. She could not blame the man. He was trying to help her. "My grandmother's."

They rode in silence. Two wagons rattled down the road toward them, each driver grim of face. "Gerta didn't leave?"

Her chin shot up. "We are nursing . . ." The wagon hit a stone, and a murmur of groans and moans saturated the air. Riley glanced over his shoulder, eyes sad. When she caught his look, he grimaced.

"They commissioned me to carry their wounded. It's all we can do."

A caisson lay shattered in the middle of the road, and Riley was forced to wait for another wagon to clear the path before passing the wreckage. *It's all we can do . . .* Hadn't she already settled that? All she could do was help. Nursing was all that was left to her.

From soldier to soldier, one bruised and bloodied man at a time, Joe moved, Jim at his side. He recognized face after face of men from his regiment. Jim helped shift men on their beds, picking up those who had fallen off the tables or cots, carrying those who had died out to the wagon parked outside the door. And always when Jim left to assist one of the surgeons or their assistants, he made sure Joe was settled and secure. "Miss Beth wouldn't like it if I let anything happen to you."

The observation seemed personal. Joe didn't dwell on it. Jim had fashioned a crutch for him to lean on when weakness would have sent him to the floor. That was when the surgeon's assistant asked the black man to make more.

There wasn't a spot anywhere not occupied by the injured, dying, or dead. The cellar had been filled long ago, Joe's cot commandeered by a captain whose leg had been amputated. He hated to think of the men down there, all but forgotten, the hope of life diminished by a quick assessment by a surgeon, assistant, or sometimes just an ambulance driver.

In every face, he searched for Ben, knowing he would not find him.

They moved farther out into the yard, Jim's strong arm helping him along. "There won't be anywhere for us to lie down tonight," Joe said as he surveyed the chaos. He let his head fall back, the sky tinged a familiar shade of red. Where had he seen that color? Surely not the bloodied body of the men . . . No. With satisfaction, he realized he had seen that shade in the blocks Beth had been sewing together.

His moment of levity was snatched away on the scream of a man and the dull, hollow sound of a saw working against flesh and bone. He grasped his right arm. The muscles in his shoulders tensed as he stood, mesmerized by the tormented victim's cries, terrified by the knowledge that it could be him. Try as he might, he could not make a fist, but his flesh was warm and he could control his arm's movements, though they were jerky and difficult.

Jim appeared at Joe's side. "Sit down. Wagon's coming and I got to help unload the men." Jim eased him to the ground. The motion broke the hold of Joe's private fear just as the surgeon finished the amputation and called for the next patient.

On either side of him, men lay in repose, eyes open, staring at nothing, some talking, while still the gaze of others grazed over him with something akin to suspicion. With a jolt he realized they would not recognize him. He wore no uniform, only the clothes of a civilian.

Jim moved away from him, and Joe relaxed against the tree as a wagon stopped. A man sprang down and hurried around to the other side. Beth. She seemed pale. Shaken. Glancing around, Joe knew the woman had seen more of the same horror. Perhaps worse if the smoke in the air were any indication of the damage the town had sustained. The man spoke to her and she nodded. A surge of men came forward and began unloading the wounded from the wagon, placing them on stretchers made of fence rails and tent canvas.

Joe stabbed the end of the crutch into the ground with as much strength as he could muster. He rallied, sucked in a deep breath, and tried to pull himself up. The world rocked and swayed before him, but he took long, slow pulls of air and everything settled. Beth was coming toward him, her expression drawn.

When he caught her gaze, she moved in his direction. Slow movements that revealed a limp.

Her hand on his arm felt warm. "What are you doing out here?"

"No room for me in the inn."

"Riley can take you somewhere else." She turned away and lifted her head. "Riley!"

The man, deep in conversation, must not have heard. Joe reached out to Beth before she could call out again. "I'll get along fine."

"You're not strong enough."

He jerked his head toward the others. "Neither are they. And you're limping."

Beth's eyes went wide. Dismay flashed across her face and she glanced away. "It's an old injury." She faced him. "But you . . ."

Looking into Beth's eyes, seeing her concern, he wanted to believe it was something else entirely. Her dark hair was mussed. Strands clung to her neck, and the image stirred the memory of another. Her eyes had been different from Beth's. Darker. For an instant, he lost himself in what his mind conjured.

"You need to rest."

He let the memory go and leaned toward her, hoping to quell her worry. "I'm not in uniform. I'll be just another injured man."

She caught on to his way of thinking and finally nodded. "Where's my grandmother?"

"Reading to some of the men in the parlor."

"Elizabeth . . ." The man who had driven the wagon stepped up beside Beth. He paused, glanced at Joe, then cleared his throat, a silent question in his eyes. Only when she faced him did he continue. "I'll come back for you and your grandmother tonight. You can't stay here."

14

No answer came to Beth. Riley waited, yet she couldn't put voice to the words. Leaving meant . . . everything. The house, the farm, was all Gerta had known for more years than Beth could count. Leaving meant no defense against the whims of the Rebels. Mr. Nisewander had understood that, though it had been a fight he had no strength for. Gerta would not either.

For the first time, she realized the bright whitewash of the house's exterior had been sheared off. Windows were shattered, or cracked. The porch sagged at an unnatural angle, though she could see no cause for it. Holes marred the wood slats. And the blood . . . What had been a bad dream of men stretched along the parlor floor had become a nightmare during the day's battle. Wounded would continue to fill up the rooms. Her room.

Rebels dragged a sack of grain from the barn and Beth knew the devastation had begun in earnest. Gerta would be left with nothing, her house and lands raped in spite of the help she so graciously offered to the very men who were pillaging. Anger rose, then cooled when she took in those around her. How many times had she seen their desperation? Sensed their weakness? They, too, were caught in the middle of life and death and their pain could not be ignored.

God would take care of Gerta. At least she'd had the good sense to send the animals away. She would not be destitute.

It was what Gerta would say. What she would believe and live by.

"It is a good idea, Beth."

She turned and searched Joe's face, saw the way Riley was watching them. She nodded and knew she had to get Gerta away if for no other reason than for rest and sleep.

"I'm not sure where we'd go."

"Your parents would welcome you." Riley climbed into the wagon. "You'll let me know when I come back."

"Yes."

She lifted her eyes to the men stretched out all around her on the lush September grasses that were now trampled. She hurried into the house, forgetting about Joe and Jim, up the stairs to her bedroom. Those fields, strewn with the injured and dying, meant she had little time to secure her belongings before the entire house was filled with more Rebels. She ducked into her grandmother's room and stripped it of personal belongings, making a similar pile in the center of her grandmother's bed on an old quilt. She picked up the bundle and returned to her room. Nothing was left except furniture. The rug had even disappeared. Only the sheet remained. She knew the mattress would soon be used by a man, maybe two or three, squeezed together on the bed. She bent to gather the four corners.

Jim shoved something at her when she reached the porch, careful of the new angle and her footing. The brown paper package of quilt blocks.

"Thought you'd want these," Jim murmured.

She pressed her lips together and nodded, hoping the man would see how much his rescue of the package and Joe's haversack meant to her. How she longed for the opportunity of quietness to take the quilt blocks out and work on adding yet another one or two to the pattern.

"Is there somewhere you can put these things?"

Jim's face creased into a smile. "Can do that quick enough. Know just the spot."

She shifted the bundle and the package into his waiting arms. Booted feet hit the porch and she retreated against the wall to make room for the stretcher bearers and their hapless burden. The men gave no apology, no acknowledgment of her presence, and the message became clear in her mind. Gerta's house had become Confederate property. She was no longer welcome.

⸺∞⸺

"You know something about wood work?" Jim asked.

Joe wiped the moisture from his upper lip, aware of the cries that clawed at his heart and mind. He'd heard the battlefield wounded many times, more than he wanted to remember, but this time, being caught in the middle of it instead of marched away to the next battle brought it home in stark clarity. He lifted the stick of wood, set to be a crosspiece on a crutch and tried to push back the light-headed feeling and focus on the black man. What was it he'd just asked? He stared at the wood in his hands.

"Joe?"

Jim was in front of him, saying something he couldn't quite catch. He felt cold where once he'd felt warm. Bile rose in his throat and he lifted on his good arm to release his stomach from the grip of nausea. Even as he lay back, eyes on the sky, weakness consumed him entirely.

106

"You've pushed too hard," Jim was saying. "You rest." The big man's hand cradled and lifted his head, then slipped something beneath it. "Miss Beth is calling for me."

Joe shut his eyes and let the sounds invade. His body relaxed into the folds of slumber, his imagination immediately rocked by the sounds of exploding shells.

The pain in his side burst open, then numbness. Ben was there, hovering over him, his lips moving, but Joe couldn't hear his words. Couldn't hear anything.

The world tilted again and they were in camp. Ben was gone and Joe moved from campfire to campfire trying to find his brother. Where was he?

Bright sunlight winked out the fires and Ben was there again, rolling his blanket, moving away as the rest of Hill's column formed up for the March. Joe looked over his shoulder, expecting to see Ben at any moment. Spotting him in the meadow they'd just left, kneeling, then up and running toward them. His smile was wide. Satisfied. There was a new cockiness in his step that Joe didn't understand.

When he next opened his eyes, his head throbbed and darkness greeted him. He was being lifted like a baby and he wanted to protest. He could walk, couldn't he?

"Ben?"

"Sh."

Jim. His name escaped him and he fell back into unconsciousness to a time when another man carried him. Hushed him.

"We take care of you but you gotta be quiet."

The voice was familiar and the words were too, but not for him. They were for the black man, the elderly man with the white hair. He'd start up yelling for no reason until the black woman with him was forced to put a gag on his mouth.

All the images bundled together in his head until sleep pulled him down farther and the dreams stopped.

15

You'll be safe here for now," Jim assured Beth and Gerta. He helped Gerta down and shouldered the bundles. Beth settled her weight onto her aching leg with care and held onto the wagon for support. She had nothing to say to Riley. He had made his decision long ago and so had she. It was water under the bridge, even if his abandonment felt more like betrayal. The wagon shifted beneath Jim's weight as he jumped into the wagon and gathered the unconscious Joe into his arms. She felt Riley's eyes shift from her, to the departing back of Jim, and back to her.

"He's one of them," Riley said.

Not Jim. Dark skin didn't bother Riley. It was Joe's presence Riley was questioning. She met his gaze head on. "He's a friend."

Even the darkness of the woods couldn't hide Riley's frown. He merely picked up the reins and started the wagon forward, down the unmarked trail.

The small log cabin deep in the woods gave a modicum of solitude from the horrors so prevalent in Sharpsburg. Gerta's reaction to leaving had been laced with relief, and Beth had known then that she had made the right decision for her grandmother.

"Why don't you lie down? I'll untie your bundle and you can use your wedding quilt." She said the words in hopes they would bring a measure of reassurance to the unusually quiet woman.

"I think I will."

Beth didn't press for answers to her worry. Gerta found a corner of the cabin and stretched out on the crude cot built into the wall. Jim had placed Joe against the wall opposite Gerta's cot before leaving to retrieve something more from the wagon. Seeing Joe's flushed face ratcheted up Beth's worries. Jim hovered at her elbow and set both her package and Joe's haversack nearby.

"He too weak to be doing all the moving he did. Couldn't tell him no though."

"You did as much as anyone could, Jim."

"If'n I know anything, it's he's got the fever."

Gerta joined them, kneeling beside the soldier. "I have nothing to offer him."

"There's that willow tree down a ways," Jim offered. "Mama brewed us tea from the bark when we was sick."

"Is there a lantern?" Beth asked.

Jim produced an old glass lantern. "Needs oil and cleaning."

"Set it here, Jim," Gerta motioned to a low stool. "Use my quilt to cover that window first."

Beth knelt beside Joe and pressed her fingertips to his forehead. He was burning up.

"Would you mind fetching that bark?" Gerta asked. "I know you're just as exhausted as we are."

"Yes, ma'am. It's not far."

Gerta sat back on her heels. "I learned much about herbs from your mama."

The knowledge drew a huge grin from the black man before he ducked through the doorway and into the night.

Gerta's fingers worked the shirt from Joe's chest as Beth got to her feet. "I'll collect wood." They had nothing except the sheet to use for fresh bandages for Joe's wound. She chided herself for not thinking more about their physical needs instead of their comfort. Especially Joe's. She nibbled the inside of her lip and wondered why it meant so much to her to have Joe with them. Because he was their first patient? The way in which he arrived? That they had already compromised him by being forced to burn the lice-infested uniform?

Joe had seemed so full of energy that afternoon, but Jim was right, he had overdone himself. Besides they needed the extra room at the house and, unless she missed her guess when looking at the bloody, rutted fields that used to be farms but now were littered with the bodies of wounded and dead, both armies would require every inch of room that could be spared.

In the quiet of darkness, she thought she could still hear the moaning of the men, but they were too far northwest of town to be close to the battlefields. Tomorrow she would return and continue to help. If only she had flour and water, the sourdough starter. Apples and carrots, the onions . . . She pushed the memory of plenty away. No use tormenting herself with what they'd had only hours ago. It was all gone now, and if not all gone, it would soon be eaten by the Rebs.

She searched the ground for sticks, kindling. Her hands hovered until her eyes adjusted enough to see the small dead branches. She returned with her treasure in tow, surprised to find Gerta wrapping a length of bandage around Joe's chest.

"Where . . . ?"

Gerta's eyes crinkled at the corners as she stood and pointed downward. A clean rip at the hem of her dress showed where

Joe's new bandage had come from. Beth's throat swelled at the magnitude and extent of her grandmother's sacrifice.

Joe woke long enough to take but a few sips of the tea. His eyelids grew heavy and he grimaced and rubbed his right side with his left hand. The new bandage must have stirred discomfort. She needed sleep, but knew it would not come easy, not with the terrible events of the day to be processed and considered.

"You were limping."

She started and met Joe's gaze, his hazy focus on her sharpened. Covering her reaction, she tried to downplay the injury. "It's nothing." What would he think if he knew she was crippled and it was permanent?

His quiet stare penetrated the wall she'd created after Riley's reaction, and the knowledge that Joe's acceptance meant more than it should. "If it hurts, then it's not 'nothing.'"

"The men need me. Need Gerta. And someone has to keep an eye on her."

The spark of a smile lifted his lips. "Is that her I hear?"

Though not overly loud, Gerta's soft snores nevertheless filled the room. Beth didn't mind. For her it was evidence that her grandmother was getting the rest she so needed. She'd been worried to see her energy waning and the paleness of her complexion growing ever more obvious.

She filled a mug with the little bit of fresh water Jim had brought in at some point. Joe lifted himself, her hand on his neck to support his head. Heat radiated from him and the effort to drink leached away the little strength he mustered.

"Will you read to me?"

Joe's quiet request seemed a perfect remedy. "I made sure to hide your haversack with our things. Jim put them up on a crossbeam in the cellar, out of sight." She grinned. "No one bothered them at all."

He blinked, long and slow. "Thank you."

Heat bloomed and began a slow creep up her neck as she realized how proud of herself she sounded. She dug in his haversack for the Bible and pulled the stool and lamp closer. A crisp sheet of paper slipped out. Joe held out his hand for it. He unfolded it and squinted, lips moving as he read. When he finished, his hand fell to his side, his mouth a firm line.

"Bad news?"

"It's a letter I was writing." He turned his face away.

She didn't know what else to say and decided it best to let the subject go. She thumbed through a few more pages of the Bible. How long had it been since she'd read from the Word? "Where do you want me to begin?"

"Galatians."

She raised her eyebrows, aware of the way he studied her. For the split second their gazes locked, he seemed at conflict with himself. "Your favorite?" she asked.

"My father used to read it to us."

Beth turned to Galatians, her fingers on the pages recalling the order of the books of the New Testament. She preferred the stories. She angled the Bible to better capture the stream of weak light and smoothed the page. The chapter introduced Paul, and then the fourth verse flowed and the words sank deep into her conscience. "Who gave himself for our sins, that he might deliver us from this present evil world, according to the will of God and our Father."

Was there anything more evil than war? Hatred that drove man against man?

"It makes me wonder why we're here," Joe inserted into the long silence. "Fighting. Dying."

A sharp stab made her sit up straight. "You are not dying."

His gaze washed over her, a small smile playing at the corners of his lips. "I'd like to live." He tried to raise his right arm. "Not much use I'll be to anyone."

"You still have a heart to give and a life to live."

Now his smile broke through. "Very poetic, and I can see that you believe it by what you're giving to us. The enemy."

She broke eye contact. Joe was a soldier. Why did his life matter so much to her? She didn't want to think about it anymore. "My father used to say that war was generated because a man took a stand for what he believed in."

"It sounds noble." He swallowed and turned his face away, but not before she saw the lines of sadness mar his brow. "Until you see it up close."

She closed the Bible. Haunting images, residue from the day's battle, drifted over her, and she didn't want to talk anymore. Yet she knew she would not sleep. The oil in the lamp was low. She picked up the lantern and lifted it to blow out the light, meeting Joe's stare. He wrestled with his own demons, and she had no answers for him, nor the strength nor the will to delve deeper. She would be out on the fields tomorrow trying to understand mercy and love in the midst of pain and despair. Joe's green eyes burned in her mind. She set the lantern aside and turned down the wick as low as she dared, a sudden need to touch something of home and family rising in her.

"You should sleep."

"As should you. Rest your leg."

"I-I won't be able to. I thought I might work on the quilt."

Beth stretched out until her fingers could grasp her bundle Jim had set nearby. She unknotted the top and stopped, realizing it wasn't the clothes or the shoes she sought, but the package from her mother. The quilt and the meaning behind the colors and squares. It was home to her, hearkening to the days when peace was a reality and her childhood innocence was intact.

She matched another square to the three, checked the length of thread, and began. It was work that focused her attention on the length of her stitches and the certainty of the next movement, and the next, never wavering from the routine until another block was added. Guilt edged every stitch as the oil in the lantern dwindled.

She blinked and realized the cabin had grown colder, that Joe slept, on his side, facing her, as if he'd been watching her for a long time.

Reaching out, she touched his tousled hair and smoothed it back from his face. He was handsome. Kind. A Rebel soldier caught in the mire of a war that had stripped him of so much. Only Jim lay awake, the whites of his eyes showing his level of alertness.

"Almost done?"

She held up the five squares. Flexed and relaxed her fingers to relieve the stress of the close work just as she'd seen her mother do countless times. "Not quite."

She splayed her hand, tracing the outline of her stitches, the subtle yet bold pattern. "Am I keeping you awake?"

"No. Just thinking. Praying. Listening."

She folded the blocks up and placed them back on the pile of personal belongings, knotting the top again, not knowing if they would be forced to move from their little hideaway in the woods or not.

Lying down next to Gerta, she settled her skirts, raked her fingers through the knots of her hair and braided it into a long tail that snaked down her back. Morning and the continued fighting would come all too soon.

16

September 18, 1862

Joe felt like he was melting from the inside out. Judging from the darkness, he guessed it must be night and he wondered what woke him. Or who. He gazed around the interior of the room and worked hard to place where he was. Memory came back in slow stages as he recalled the house, the wounded. Gerta and Jim. Beth. She sat beside him and leaned into his line of vision.

"Bad dream?"

He ran his tongue over dry lips. Every move felt like he'd been out in the blazing sun too long.

Beth dipped a cloth into water and wrung it out. Water trickled back into the basin. Joe could only think how good the water would taste. He was so hot.

The coolness of the cloth felt like a chill winter breeze against his skin and he welcomed it even as gooseflesh rose on his arms. Meredith would not welcome such trivial tasks. She would hate caring for the wounded—really, for anyone other than herself.

Joe tried to place the name with the face, and how he would know such a personal thing about someone. Details danced just out of range of his throbbing head. He tried to raise his hand to his head but his fingers touched something stiff. Paper. In the semidarkness, he raised the single sheet and a flood of memory came back as he recognized the paper as the letter he'd been writing home to Meredith.

The debutante intent on defying her father by marrying a man below her station. He'd been flattered and awed by her fragile beauty. Her father thought him an opportunist taking advantage of his wayward daughter's affections.

> Dearest Meredith,
>
> The war is nothing as I thought it would be. I'm sure there are many other men who feel the same. Ben and I camp tonight in a meadow outside of Frederick. Tomorrow we move out toward a gap in South Mountain and on toward Hagerstown.
>
> As I'm sure you do not want to hear the details of daily life, I'll exclude them from this letter.

It was as far as he had gotten, not knowing what else to say. She was lovely, but shrewd and cunning and he suspected he was more a toy for the spoiled girl to cling to in spite of her father's demand to surrender it, than a man to be loved and honored. Around campfires when there was nothing to do and another battle was imminent, the men talked of home to keep their minds off the possibility of death that stared them between the eyes. He'd heard his friends speak of their girls, the love and longing evident in their voices. Why didn't he feel like that? How was it he had so easily forgotten who should be the most important person to him?

He didn't need to linger too long over the question. Meredith had been a mistake. He'd known it when he was penning the letter just as he realized it now. He'd known for some time the reality of the relationship. Realized that Meredith didn't really expect a proposal nor want one—she simply adored the attention and stirring her father's anger.

Compared to what he saw in Gerta and in Beth, Meredith's pledge of love lost its value. She would expect a lifestyle he could not provide and she would come to hate him, or demand that he acquiesce and go to work for her father.

"Would you like me to put that away for you?"

He rolled his head toward Beth. "It's a letter."

"I see that."

"I need to finish it." The very words he'd spoken were like a benediction. He folded the letter and rested it on his stomach, wondering what he would say. How to say it . . .

"Are you right-handed?"

Beth provided the very excuse he needed. He would release Meredith knowing she would not endure a man rendered a cripple.

"I can finish it for you."

He knew it was the right thing to do, but doing it, actually breaking off the relationship with Meredith, left him with nothing. Not Ben. Not his mother . . . He closed his eyes and swallowed against the surge of emotion. "Maybe later."

I'm all alone.

The cloth was on his face again. His neck. His cheeks. It felt so good. He opened his eyes briefly and caught Beth's soft gaze. She was disheveled and tired-looking, but her eyes held such a kindness and understanding. As if she could read his heart and mind. Her hand stilled and she drew back, sitting up straight. Joe's heart pounded harder and he wondered if it was the fever, or his mind playing tricks on him, but when Beth's hand slipped into his, he didn't feel so alone anymore.

Beth sat back, flushed. As soon as Joe's eyes closed, she chided herself for thinking something had changed in Joe's warm, green eyes. He was feverish. Delirious, more than likely. Yet he'd been talking clearheaded . . . She quashed the errant flow of her thoughts even as his fingers squeezed hers and his breathing evened out as evidence of sleep.

It meant nothing.

She sighed and slipped her hand from his. Her eyes landed on the single sheet of paper and curiosity drew her to unfold it. He seemed to dread the idea of finishing it and she wondered if she should simply sit down and write it for him. Let the person know that he was recovering from a wound that had left his right hand weakened.

My dearest Meredith

The words jumped out at her, accusing. She tamped back the panic. Meredith could be anyone. A sister. The rest of the letter didn't mention anything that would give a clue, though she couldn't help the spark of satisfaction that it, at least, didn't seem overly personal. Maybe Meredith was nothing more than a family friend.

She folded the letter back and felt the first spike of heat in her cheeks. She'd had no business reading something so personal without his knowledge, even if he had seemed open to the idea of her finishing the letter. She smoothed the stiff paper, then put it back in the haversack for safekeeping.

Jim returned as the sun grew hotter with an armful of produce, fresh from the ground judging by the mud clinging to the carrots. The women didn't ask and neither did Joe, where Jim had gotten the food or the berries. They ate with thankfulness and need, the women making sure Joe and Jim had the bigger portions. What they didn't eat Jim stored under a floorboard, along with a fresh supply of willow bark.

Beth made Joe drink a tea made of the bark. He felt no better than before, but no worse either. Just weak and sick. Not even the little bit of food Gerta forced on him seemed to relieve the weakness. Gerta fussed over his shoulder for a long time. After taking off the bandage, she'd frowned over the wound and he feared what the dark look meant. He didn't ask.

Silence stretched long as tension pulled at each of them. They rested, waiting for Riley to arrive, expecting a shell to destroy the blessed silence accompanied by the rattle of guns and screams of war. Already worn nerves stretched tighter.

Joe pushed himself to stay awake. He needed to get stronger. To force his muscles to work as they should. Jim fashioned another crutch, notching the crosspiece and he offered to help. He found that though he couldn't grip the wood, his arm could trap it and hold it still while his left hand worked. The work was tedious and frustrating but he forced himself to do it for much the same reason he suspected Gerta had gone in search of more herbs and Beth huddled over the quilt blocks, her needle rising and falling. Work was normal and a diversion from worry.

He rested against the wall at his back and let himself enjoy the weak sunshine and quiet. "Where are we?"

Jim stopped working on forming the long, smooth stick. "In the woods northeast of Sharpsburg."

Beth continued to sew, oblivious to his stare or his question. He admired the way her dark hair shone in the stream of sunshine. He smiled at the messy braid that lay over her shoulder. She was beautiful. An angel. Her selflessness matched that of her grandmother and he wondered if it was that easy to become enamored of a nurse.

Joe turned his head and saw Jim's sober expression merge into a sly lifting of the corners of his mouth. Joe ducked his head. It wasn't hard to know what the black man must have thought catching him staring at Beth like that. He smoothed over the wood caught beneath his right arm, determined he would not look up again.

"You're feeling better?" Jim asked, a trace of amusement in his voice.

"Some." And he did. Just the act of sitting up had helped. He still felt hot, but determined to help Jim instead of sleeping. He tried to lift his right arm. What had been numbness the previous day in his arm had become a burning sensation today. He wondered if Gerta's care of the wound had helped.

"I've known about this cabin for a long time. Knew it would be a good place to go," Jim offered.

"Why didn't you leave me back with the rest of them?"

Jim's eyes widened, his glance back at Beth seemed to say something. "You're not in uniform and you saved the others. Didn't seem right to leave you when staying might mean you'd lose that arm."

He suspected Jim's reasoning left a deeper story untold but he didn't press.

"It might be wise for you to stay here with him, Jim."

Joe swung his head toward Beth, gulped at the picture of loveliness she made, haloed by the light. He lowered his eyes. This was no time to mire his emotions with another woman. Not when he still had to decide about Meredith. And then there was Ben's death . . .

All at once, he lost what little strength he'd had. He could feel the room begin a slow spin. Jim was beside him, guiding him down. Beth, too, fussed. Her hands against his cheeks. He didn't want to think anymore, but when he closed his eyes the trickle of images became a torrent.

He was being dragged by Ben, wounded, bleeding. They had sought refuge in the woods in a dilapidated structure not more than a shack with a narrow loft. They'd huddled there, Ben working over his wound when they heard shuffling, muffled voices, and a man's tormented scream. They had stumbled upon the hiding place of three blacks—a woman, a man, and an older man who was losing his mind and slowing them down. They were lost and fearful and so close to the North. Ben had sought to reassure them that he could help them.

In the dark of the night, they'd led them from the shack. A figure loomed up in front of them, gun aimed at them. Ben backed up a step, grunted his name and rank, but shots rang out, catching Ben. Twisting him. His face contorted and Joe's muscles tensed as he reached to catch his brother. There was a wrench of pain in his shoulder as his own wound did not bear the stress and broke open. For a brief moment he'd stared up at the shooter. One glimpse before the man turned and walked away.

Joe gasped and stiffened, the memory shattering. He cradled his head in his hand, a cry stabbing from his throat.

"Joe?"

He opened his eyes to Beth's concerned face and didn't know what to say, even as the image snapped into place, heavy with truth. A Confederate had killed his brother. Shot him dead right before Joe's eyes. He drew air into his lungs, unable to speak. Felt himself lifted, or was he falling?

"Joe?"

Beth hovered over him, those beautiful eyes filled with anxiety. Her hands smoothed over his face and he longed to grasp them, to still them so they could not distract him. He had to think. The last piece of the puzzle was there. Out of reach, slipping away even as he tried to rein it closer and force it to yield its secret. "Why didn't you shoot me?"

"Sh."

His hand clamped down on Beth's wrist. She had to understand. "Why didn't he shoot me too?"

Confusion marred Beth's features, or was that pain? Jim's hand peeled his fingers from Beth's wrists, pressed him back onto the ground. "You'll not be hurting, Miss Beth."

Hurting? Had he hurt her? He hadn't meant to, it was just that the memory cut so deep. He turned his face away from them both.

<hr />

Gerta leaned over Joe, eyes missing nothing in her quick assessment. "He should sleep now." She sat back on her heels. "I agree with Beth, Jim. The less you're seen the better."

Beth rubbed at her left wrist, shocked both by the tightness of Joe's grip and the desperation in his voice. Who should have shot him? It was like he saw her but didn't see her.

"Fever does this sometimes. Makes them see things that aren't there. And he's been through so much . . ." Gerta said as she rolled to her knees. Jim aided her to her feet. "Sometimes dreams trap a person." Her expression filled with compassion as she watched Joe's sleeping form. "We can only imagine the horrors these men have witnessed."

A squeaking rattle came from outside. Riley was approaching the shack. Beth didn't want to leave Joe. But the grim expression on Riley's face, coupled with Gerta's tizzied roundup of the herbs she'd collected that morning, reinforced her will.

"Riley?" Gerta's question wore heavy on the man, demanding an explanation for the distress pinching his features.

"It's much worse than we thought. The heat of day will not help and we cannot move fast enough. Some are dying where they lie." Riley averted his face and Beth could see his fight to retain his composure. With slow movements, he came to the side of the wagon and offered his hand to Gerta. "They torched the Mummas'. The house and barn are gone. Along Hog Trough there is nothing but . . ."

Gerta patted Riley's hand before planting her foot to haul herself onto the wagon seat. She paused and met Beth's gaze.

It was the deciding moment. Her grandmother was asking something of her. Based on what she'd seen the previous day, Beth wasn't at all sure she could go out onto those fields, criss-crossed with dilapidated fences and view up close the devastation she'd only seen at a distance the previous day.

Despite the rest of the night, strain and fatigue showed in Gerta's face. "I would like to see," Gerta said a moment before she pulled herself into the wagon and settled her tattered, blood-stained skirt around her ankles. Gerta sat prim, as if dressed in her Sunday best and ready for a nice buggy ride. The stoop of her shoulders and lines of strain around her mouth the only sign of the woman's discomfort.

Nurses were expected to offer comfort and help the wounded. It was on this battlefield that Beth would receive the majority of her training. Her stomach knotted with dread. Gerta's gaze went over her, her face placid, calm. If her grandmother could do it, surely she could as well. If she could offer comfort to one man, as she had to Joe, it would ease the darkness that had inhabited her soul since Leo's death.

Beth shifted her weight. Riley waited, expectant, offering his hand, and all she could think about was her mother's expression, her sadness. The way her parents looked at her. Sometimes it felt as though they were looking right through her. She closed her eyes and envisioned the quilt, the colorful triangles against the dark background, leading, pointing, to something bright and wonderful.

But she had to continue the journey. She'd taken the first step by nursing the many Confederates brought to their door. No. She'd taken the first step by overcoming her anger to take care of Joe. It was up to her to continue the journey toward that bright hope. Whatever it was. She wanted it, needed to feel the hope she had once felt, and though she didn't understand, she knew that this was yet another step on the path.

She glanced at Jim.

"You go on. I'll take good care of Joe."

Embarrassed that Jim so easily read her worry, she allowed Riley to help her into the wagon and settled her skirts over her bad leg, never once looking back at the cabin or Jim.

17

Joe's head throbbed and he stroked his fingers along his brow to relieve the tension that had settled behind his eyes. He remembered his dream about Ben and groaned. The cabin had grown as hot as he felt, the beams of sunlight creeping along the floor ever closer to him with each passing minute. He heard a movement and expected to feel Beth's fingers along his face, testing for fever, instead Jim's voice cut through his misery.

"You hungry?"

"No." He'd been so used to low rations, or no rations, of fending for himself along the March into the Shenandoah Valley. The steady supply of food had been more than he'd had in a long time.

"Miz Gerta says the fever makes you say crazy things. You hurt Miss Beth with asking why they didn't shoot you, too."

He remembered none of it save the dream. Or was it a dream? But he recalled it play-by-play and knew it was yet another piece of his memory's puzzle. "Someone shot my brother."

"Who?"

"I don't know."

"They said he saved their lives. That you did. It was the reason they risked theirs for you."

Joe's head snapped up. Jim continued to run his knife down the long branch he was smoothing for another crutch. He had risked his life for . . . who? *The slaves.* How he wished he could have known them, their names. He wondered how far they had dragged him. No matter how hard he tried, he couldn't recall anything after Ben was shot until he woke up in Gerta's home.

"We found them in the woods."

"Where was you?"

"Over the mountain."

"Well, you Rebs lost that one from what I've heard. It's why you're here. The Graybacks overwhelmed Harper's Ferry though."

He could rouse himself to be happy for the men of his regiment. The extra clothes and shoes, guns and ammunition would have been a God-send.

"Where'd you get shot?"

Joe rolled to his good side, facing the black man and watching the slow move of his hands back and forth with the blade of his pocketknife.

They'd been marching toward that gap in the mountain from the meadow outside of Frederick. He and Ben had been caught in a skirmish with five others. He told Jim as much. They'd been in the woods somewhere halfway up the mountain, Ben nursing his shoulder in the little shack.

"Why didn't he take you to one of your surgeons?"

"I think he was, but we ran into the slaves and . . ."

"So who shot him?"

"I don't know." The image of that man, his face so cold. As if he'd planned the shot all along. Like a mercenary seeking revenge. Why hadn't he been shot as well? Why only Ben?

"I want to remember, but I can't."

"Them blacks said it was a dark man. Had a gray coat and blue pants."

"You talked to them?"

"Heard tell."

Joe didn't know what to make of the Jim's vague response but didn't push the issue. What interested him most was the information. Gray coat and blue pants. He tried to reconcile his image of the man with the clothing and felt another missing piece slip into place. Desperate as the men were for clothing, he could see them putting on almost anything to be rid of the smelly, mud-caked, and sweat-soaked rags. Maybe the man had been Union after all. Still, it didn't make sense that he would shoot Ben and leave him alive.

He turned onto his back and let his mind drift. A cold, hard truth edged itself into his mind. The man who shot Ben had known his brother. He was after Ben and only Ben.

No matter how hard he tried to make sense of it, he failed.

"You thought about what you going to do? Don't see how they'll be wanting you back with a busted arm."

In response to the statement, Joe tried to flex his right hand as he contemplated an answer. His injury could be his ticket out of the Army of Northern Virginia, and the thought had never been sweeter. He'd seen enough, done enough. More than a year into the war had ground down many a man. Ben had talked of ending the war. Of heading home and picking up where they had left off in their humble carriage-making shop. But the injury would limit Joe's capacity to work. He would head home to a trade that he was no longer able to work, and that was if the shop survived further battles as the Union tried to press south just as the South tried to press north.

There would be nothing he could do. Nowhere he could go to escape the crude existence forced on him because of his injury.

"She cares for you, you know."

Joe froze up inside. He lifted his head and Jim's calm dark eyes stared back. He hadn't wanted to read too much into Beth's reaction to him. They were both so vulnerable. All of them. And then there was the other: "I'm a Rebel."

"You're a man first."

"My arm's no good."

"You'll find something you can do."

Why were they even having this discussion? "It's why you brought me with you, isn't it?"

Jim's eyes crinkled at the corners but he didn't respond, only slipped from his stool to the floor and pressed the piece he had been whittling into Joe's right hand. "Grip this."

Joe did, squeezing with all his might.

"Do it again."

He tried. With every ounce of strength, he tried to get his hand to obey his mind and clench.

"Another one."

Joe glanced once at Jim. The black man's expression gave away none of his thoughts.

"Only way to keep it strong is to make it work."

"I can't."

"Not now. But you keep trying and it might get stronger."

Joe drew in a deep, settling breath. He felt so weak. Sweat beaded along his forehead as he clenched, then relaxed his hand against the smooth wood that lay in the palm of his hand.

Low laughter grated against Beth's ears, as if the soldiers themselves were testing the waters of mirth in a landscape so stained with death. The urge to turn on the men and berate them for their lightheartedness rose. She bit her lip to keep from lashing out as the wagon rattled down from Sharpsburg and they took a left onto Main. Buildings were burned. Dead horses, smashed wagons, buildings still smoldering from the fires of the previous day. Civilians stood out on the streets, some kneeling next to fallen men, others wandering, their expressions glazed with pain and confusion.

The Lutheran church's whitewashed sides were skinned and riddled with holes. Across the street, a surgeon had set up a coarse tent, the telltale pile of limbs drawing flies in the heat of the day. A whimper rose in her throat and she determined not to look anymore. Every fiber of her being wanted to beg Riley to turn around and take her back to the shack, away from the gore and wreckage and buzz of flies.

Only her grandmother's stiff carriage and steady forward gaze settled her nerves and firmed her resolve. Stretched out in front of them was the mess she'd glimpsed the previous evening, only worse. A picket stopped them, shooting questions at Riley as to his intentions. They were waved through, the lone horse continuing its plod down the dirt road littered on both sides with broken fence rails. Entire sections of the five-rail fence were missing in some places.

Beth closed her eyes as the cacophony of moans and shrieks of the injured and dying grew in volume. She felt Gerta's hand on hers and squeezed back.

"It is far worse than even I imagined."

"I'm not strong enough for this."

Her grandmother's hand squeezed tighter. "You would want someone to care for Jedidiah. Each of these men is a Jedidiah to someone somewhere. Don't focus on the injury, many will

129

be too far gone to hear your words, but they can feel your presence. You might be able to say something that will bring them peace as they cross over."

Her mind rejected the thought. She who had no peace was to bring peace to others? The idea seemed absurd.

"How can I when . . ."

Gerta's hand squeezed. "You'll find the strength when you need it most. Pray, my darling. God has not turned His back on you. Just as He did not turn His back on Leo."

She tilted her head and blinked into the clear blue sky. Such a beautiful blue, a glory lost to those whose eyes stared up into it unseeing, abandoned.

18

Joe worked his hand on the crosspiece in increments of ten before he rested. He was alone. Jim had slipped off to somewhere. In the warmth of the cabin, Joe pulled his haversack close. He rubbed the place where the wound alternately itched and burned. More than anything, he wished for a cool stream and a slab of soap, but it would be a luxury he would have to defer for the unforeseen future.

He worked the buckle of the sack and opened the flap. He lifted out his letter to Meredith and set it aside. Then, one by one he took out the things Beth had so carefully showed him before. He'd had paper and an inkwell at some point. Maybe gone now, he didn't know. He knew and had seen the looting on both sides of the army upon those who had fallen in the field. Desperate soldiers in want of shoes or stamps or food.

As he ran his hand around the inside of the haversack, his finger caught on the inside edge where a hole used to be, the result of an excited mouse after his hardtack and peanuts. His finger grazed along the stitches he'd painstakingly worked to patch the hole, adding a second piece of material on the inside to form a pocket of sorts meant to hold his small wooden box. He withdrew the slender wooden case and opened it. The pen lay inside, two nibs, an inkwell, and a couple of sheets of paper. He frowned as he lifted out the paper. A cigar lay at the bottom of the narrow area with another sheet of paper underneath.

The cigar smelled rich, still retaining the freshness that bespoke of a recent purchase. Joe turned it over, trying to understand where it had come from and to whom it belonged. He didn't smoke. Ben smoked cigars before the war had begun, an infrequent indulgence, but one his brother had discontinued as soldier's pay had grown more irregular and needs for food and raiment became higher priority.

He unfolded the single sheet of paper and noted the watermark, but the page was blank. Ben must have stowed some of his goods inside Joe's haversack to free his hands.

Joe pulled himself into a sitting position and waited for the world to stop spinning. He clutched the cigar, the paper open on his lap, the realization that these were the last things of Ben's that he would ever hold until he returned home. If he returned home. He had come close to death, as had many, but Ben's death sucked away his desire to continue the fight. There was nothing more worth fighting for.

Jim's words echoed back to him. Beth. Did she truly care for him? He glanced at the chair on which she'd sat earlier, sewing. The quilt was there, flashing its message. Hope. Was God giving him a new hope?

The door creaked open an inch allowing bright sunshine to stream inside, filtered as it was though the trees, it still forced Joe to squint and turn away.

"It's me. Found us more food. They's about to eat us out of everything. The fields is ripped near clean."

Joe knew all about such things. Despite Lee's command to the contrary, pillaging meant the difference between starvation and survival. Joe put the cigar back into the bottom of the case and replaced the paper, his own sheets of paper on top, and closed the box. He picked up the crosspiece of wood and began his exercise again. He caught Jim's grin of approval as the man carried his stash of staples to a low table and set them out like a mama parading her finery. They ate the berries Jim had brought back and split some crackers and preserves. He wondered where the man had found the things but didn't ask. It was enough to have food in his belly and to feel an increment of strength he hadn't felt earlier.

"You're getting better," Jim nodded his head.

"Not as hot."

"That's a good thing. Sometimes last three, four days. I was praying God would heal you."

He didn't know what to say. Jim sounded a lot like his mother.

Jim waved his hand over the plenty in front of them. "They's about took everything already, but I hid some things yesterday, thinking them Rebs might eat us out of it all."

At least the man had foresight, but what he wanted to know most was about the battle itself. "Is it bad?"

"Most of the men I saw were bad off. Even the barn is full of men, Union and Rebs. Thought Miz Gerta and Miss Beth might be there, but they must have gone down into the fields."

Joe closed his eyes. No one had to tell him what that experience was like and he really didn't want the reminder. He wondered if it was easier for someone like Beth to see the carnage than it was for a soldier to see it and know he might be next. Or to linger near a friend knowing he would bleed to death before anyone got to him.

"That Miz Gerta is something. She been a neighbor to Mister Nisewander for a good long time."

"Mr. Nisewander?" The cranky man? "Is he your master?"

Jim's frown was dark and deep. "Ain't got no master. I'm a free man. I work for the Mister because he's a good man. Treats me fair and pays me good."

"Where is he?"

"Went down with my Emma to the cave. Best place for him all along, though it took that shelling to convince him." Jim pulled on his lone suspender, lips pursed.

"Emma is your wife?"

"My daughter."

"There's a cave around here?"

"Killiansburg Cave. Lots of folks went there to hide from the Rebs." Jim nodded toward the branch he'd been working on. "Took them crutches over and left them. Didn't like the way I was being eyeballed by the Rebs."

Jim knelt and pried up a loose board in the floor. He handed down the jars of preserves, returned to the table, caught up the bag of sweet potatoes, and stashed them along with another wrapped item and the apples. He stood up and brushed the dust from the knees of his trousers, taking another pluck at his suspender. For several long minutes, Jim said nothing, only stared down at the floor.

"Think everything will be safe there?" Joe finally asked.

"If we're careful, and if we try to stretch out what we got, we should be fine for a week, maybe more."

A week of food seemed like a luxury to Joe. He clenched the piece of wood in his right hand, realizing as he did so that the clench of his hand felt tighter. Maybe it was a trick of his imagination. "I thought you were worried about going out with Rebs in the town."

Jim shrugged. "I'm a free man. Not much they can do. Mostly saw them and heard their talk, not the other way 'round."

"What're they saying?"

"Worrying over food and supplies. The barn was filled up. The yard, too. I had to work hard to get to the well."

Ah. "So that's where you stored everything?"

"Wasn't used any more, and it was a cool place."

Jim returned to the door and glanced over his shoulder. "I'll get some more branches."

Joe set aside the crosspiece, the tendons in his arms sparking stabs of soreness. He was glad for the feeling. Anything other than numbness was welcome and maybe Jim was right, if the exercise helped him regain use of his hand it was worth the effort. He swung himself to his knees and maintained the position until he was sure the world would not tilt or spin. Left hand against the wall, he planted his right foot and pulled to his feet. His first step was shaky and he remembered the crutch Jim had given him but it was nowhere in sight. The black man had probably taken it along to the hospitals.

Winded after a dozen steps, he felt the strength waning from his legs and went for the low stool. As he crouched over it, the blood pounded hard in his head, then drained. The world shifted and he missed, hitting the edge and plopping onto the floor. He sat, dazed as pain pulsed in his right side. At least he was back on the ground. With what little strength he could muster, he got up on his hands and knees to crawl back to his side of the shack.

The door swung wide open. Joe could see Jim's wide, staring eyes taking in the room, then the place where he knelt, poised to crawl. "You fall over?"

"I walked. When I tried to sit down, I missed."

Jim's face broke into a wide smile, prelude to the belly laugh that tweaked a smile from Joe. Levity expanded his lungs and he added his own chuckle as he began to crawl, imagining what he must have looked like as he fell and, now, crawling around like an overgrown baby while trying to keep weight off his injured arm. The laughter felt good, unusual. It seemed like months ago when he'd last laughed.

"Got some strong branches right outside the door. I'll break them and we'll get started."

Jim's head lifted, tilted, eyes growing serious. Joe listened but heard nothing.

Jim's frown deepened. "Someone's coming."

19

New streaks of blood had been added to Gerta's skirts, Joe noted. Both she and Beth were pale and sober. Jim closed the door behind them as Riley set off back to the fields. Gerta went straight to the place where she'd lain the previous night and stretched out on top of a quilt. Beth acknowledged both of them, her own apron smeared with blood, her hem ragged, hair falling in stray tendrils around her face, staring at nothing. It was like she was seeing something else not entirely pleasant. She looked, to Joe's eye, near to collapse.

It was the horror of the battlefield. He knew it. She had seen what he had grown used to seeing and it was as traumatizing and terrifying as he'd known it to be for all the months he'd marched and pulled the trigger at men with families and loved ones that would never see that man's return.

He swallowed, wishing his legs were stronger, that he could bounce to his feet and touch the hair around her face. If only there was a way to protect her from it all, just as his mother and Sue had never had any protection. A hot brand of guilt seared with the knowledge that he had brought this to their doorstep. As if the direction of the entire war lay on his shoulders.

Jim scooted the stool closer to her. She sagged onto the seat like every muscle in her body had suddenly gone flaccid.

"I brought some water in," Jim offered. He didn't wait for an answer, but brought a tin mug to her. She took two sips and handed it back with a motion of her head toward Gerta.

The older woman rose long enough to take a deep drink. She spoke to Jim in tones so low Joe couldn't make out the words. Gerta's hand fluttered often to her left shoulder and massaged the spot, her face twisted with discomfort. Joe turned his attention back to Beth. Her eyes were on him. He froze, something deep inside him connecting with what he witnessed in the soberness of her eyes. Such sorrow etched in the softness of her face. Every curve translated the trauma of the day.

He braced his hand against the wall, determined to go to her, but she was there, beside him, as he gained his feet. She steadied his weight and when he glanced down, her face was inches from his. His mouth went dry as he let himself drink in the beauty of her skin, the perfection that was her nose, the eyes so clouded with the heavy load laid upon her shoulders. He could at least share it with her, bear the burden as she had born the burden of his convalescence.

Aware of the dirt and grime of the past days, the staleness of his clothes, he pulled back. "I'm afraid the air would be sweeter elsewhere."

Her grip on his hand didn't falter, a wan smile prelude to the argument that settled the issue. "We could all use a bath and a cake of strong lye soap." She took a step forward, waited for him to follow suit. He appreciated the slow pace she set, could feel her own struggling limp in the unevenness of her weight against him.

To his surprise, she opened the door. The air swirled around him, tinted with a scent he recognized. He'd done enough battlefield grave duty not to identify the smell of rot. She helped lower him to the single wooden step. He braced his back against the wall, pleased with himself, but the pleasure was crushed when she sat next to him, her shoulders slumped forward, head bowed low.

He waited, hoping she would talk to him. "I'm feeling stronger. Jim said he prayed for me."

"What about all of them? What about those who pray and don't get better?" A shudder wracked her body. "It was horrible."

He thought about all he'd lost. "My mother often reminded us that Sue's death meant heaven. A better place." And at the time it had been his mother's talk. A comfort to him, yes, but he'd never thought of her religion as his own.

Until now. Death, he realized, stared them all in the face. Every day. Every breath. Every minute. "Sometimes I think the pain of dying must show what is truly in a person's heart." Hadn't he heard that Christ had suffered before his death?

"It seems so senseless," her voice was dead. Heavy. Her head bowed into her hands. "So . . . vile."

"I guess it is, unless you're ready to go."

She had felt a deep need to talk about the horrors she had witnessed, knowing Joe would understand. Instead, the change in subject to God ground away the wall she'd held around herself since Leo's death. She rubbed her leg, aching from the uneven pocks along the battlefield and the miles she'd walked going from one destroyed soldier to another. Some alive, some not.

How did the men endure what she'd seen? Even the survivors walked around in a daze searching for fallen comrades.

She'd heard their sobs. Seen mothers and fathers being guided to the field, their faces masks of expectation and defeat. The heat, the flies, the moans and screams of those who still needed tending and had yet to be moved.

"We went along one lane where they were digging beneath those who had died to get to those who were still alive." It had been their first stop among many. Until Beth realized Gerta's color had faded, that there was a grayness around her lips. She had coaxed Gerta to go back to the shack, but she'd refused, agreeing only to stay at a field hospital where at least the men were laid out in neat rows and all alive if not conscious.

"I thought I could handle it after seeing the men at the house, but it was the . . ." She couldn't find the word.

"Seeing so many at once?"

Her throat burned. "How do you do it? March and fight and . . . kill?"

He didn't know how he had done it. He'd pulled the trigger again and again, knowing his primary goal was to stop the enemy by any method. He bowed his head. Ben had wanted so much to join the army. His brother's goading and enthusiasm had been bolstered by Sue's death and the talk of states' rights. He massaged that line between his brows where an ache throbbed. "I don't think anyone knows. You just do it."

"It's not right. It's—"

A breeze ruffled the leaves of the trees and washed over him, accompanied, again, by the faint scent of sourness and rot. Joe squeezed the bridge of his nose and tried to push away the pictures that flashed through his memory. Too awful to tell or talk about, and yet she'd seen the same thing today, up close.

His father would point him to his faith, but faith in what? The answer washed over him as if his mother had whispered the single syllable in his ear. *God.* The Bible his mother had given him was a map to something bigger than himself. He needed to feel there was something bigger than himself and in control when he felt so confused and angry and disgusted. He realized he had to let go of it all or the dwelling on it would destroy him. Ben, the men he had called friends, all of them would have died in vain if he became nothing more than a hollow shell, disillusioned with life. No, he was disillusioned with war. He couldn't change the hearts of others, but his own he could.

Beth shifted, and the movement brought him back to her and her obvious distress. She had it right. She and Gerta. Help those who could not help themselves. Minister to them. Offer comfort and a chance to be at peace before death claimed them, or hope for another tomorrow.

"What you're doing is a gift to the wounded." When she faced him, her expression was a mask of anger that chilled him. Her twisted brow, the way she held herself erect, the harshness of her frown.

"I don't see how reading a Scripture or writing a letter, or listening to a prayer is enough."

"Not enough for them, or for you?"

Her face blanched and she presented her back, rigid and unyielding.

"Who are you to say anything? You're a Rebel. The enemy. You've probably killed—"

The accusation lodged in his heart. Never had she spoken so harshly to him, and her words roused his anger. "And you are a Northerner. A lady. A woman who probably knows men and boys who have joined up with McClellan. And they are shooting at us, too."

He wanted nothing more than to leave her to her own thoughts and rid himself of further debate. There was no winning solution. Nothing he would be able to say would soften her opinion of him and with that came the realization that they could never have a future. Jim might have thought Beth had feelings for him, but they couldn't jump the fence of her prejudices against the South. He only wished he had seen sooner that she would hold against him the label of Southerner. "I watched my brother die. You are not the only one who stands to lose, Beth. I cannot change what happened before the war, and I'm sorry for you, but do not think for a minute that just because I am on the other side of this conflict that it erases my ability to love and be loved by others. Or to feel hurt and loss. I grieve as you do, for my brother and sister, and my mother and father. Grief does not select its target based on which side is fighting. We all suffer, whether before the war, during it, or after. It makes no difference."

20

Beth heard Joe's grunt to stand. She knew he was struggling to get up the step and back into the cabin. And it wasn't because he wanted to go back inside, but because of her. She squeezed her eyes shut, the anger draining away and leaving her weak and sad. She had lashed out at him as if where he was from made any difference. His words choked every bit of her own bias out of her. She was no better than him, and he was no better than her. They were two people trying to figure out their place in a world that had gone crazy with shooting and hatred and the desire to conquer.

And she was just as bad. If witnessing the pain of the wounded and dying so troubled her, how must Joe feel having lived with it every day since becoming a soldier. What she couldn't reconcile herself to was his desire to shoot another man. To pull the trigger because it was mandated.

But Jedidiah was somewhere doing the same thing. For all she knew, he could have been the one to shoot Joe's brother, or Joe, for that matter.

"Beth?" Gerta's hand was a light weight against her shoulder. Her grandmother skirted around her and settled herself on the step beside her. "Joe seemed angry when he came in. What happened?"

"He's a Rebel, Grandmama. The enemy."

Gerta blew a breath that swept the hair off her forehead. "The same old argument."

"You dismiss it so easily! Well I can't. I won't."

Her grandmother traced the ground with her eyes. She leaned forward to pluck a blade of grass from a sparse patch. "Is this about the unfairness of those who are dead and dying and those doing the killing, or is this about Leo and your injury?"

Her throat thickened and she pressed a hand to her lips. "Neither."

"So this has nothing to do with God or your idea that He took away your happiness?"

Hot rage flowed upward, threatened to overflow. She staunched a sob, the burst of temper that threatened to ride out on a scream. No one understood. They were all in this together and no one except her saw the unjustness? Did the man missing an eye and a good portion of his jaw, to whom she had knelt and read Scripture at his request, deserve what he had gotten? What about the man whose screams pierced their ears all morning—because he couldn't feel legs that the surgeon had already amputated?

"Men do what they think is right. We all do. If they fight, they realize that they also might be shot and killed, or maimed. Did you see the boy this afternoon?"

She had. A small boy, no more than fourteen, shot in the gut and crying his eyes out because he would never see his mother again.

"He told me he ran away. He thought his father wouldn't let him join because he was afraid to lose him, and then the boy told me to tell his father *he* was afraid." Gerta's voice whispered out into the growing shadows of night. She winced, hand over her heart, pressing.

"Grandmama?" Beth had seen Gerta's discomfort throughout the afternoon.

Her grandmother patted Beth's leg and Beth closed her hand over Gerta's soft one, fingers cold in spite of the heat. Gerta continued as if the conversation had never been interrupted. "Paul was his name. He told me he was named after his father." Gerta breathed deeply and slowly and fingered the ragged hem of her skirt. "I asked him what he what he wanted me to do for him and he wanted me to pray that God would forgive him for being so mean to his father and mother."

Men had begged her to write letters to their loved ones. She had done her best to meet their requests and make sure she knew their identity so she could tell the families where to find their bodies. Confederate or Union, it was always the same request. No one wanted to die alone. Only a few soldiers cursed foul words down on the enemy, the war, an old rival, as they drew their last.

"You can fight God's will, or you can trust."

"I am trusting. I've had no choice but to trust Him."

"Really?" Gerta's eyes burned into hers. "Is trust fear and hatred? Walking in darkness and shunning the light?"

Beth's heart slammed in unadulterated rage. Of all people, Gerta should understand. Her voice shuddered. "I didn't ask for this."

"For what, Bethie?"

The use of her childhood nickname sucked the rage from her. This was her grandmother. "For the war to come here. For Jedidiah to leave me or . . ." She bit down hard.

"Or for Leo to die or your leg to be crushed. No one in their right mind asks for trouble, but sometimes it is measured out to us to prove what we are made of."

"I don't want to talk about this."

Gerta patted her shoulder and rose. "I love you, Beth."

The words were there on the tip of her tongue, poised to be spoken, yet she could not push them out. Instead, she pulled her knees to her chest and pillowed her head. Tears should have streamed down her face, instead she felt nothing but a cold fierceness.

Whatever had passed between the two women, Gerta returned looking the worse for it. She fussed over Joe for a few minutes, declaring his temperature almost normal and the brevity of his fever a miracle, then retreated to her corner of the cabin. Jim hovered over her for a few minutes, trying to coax the woman to eat, coming away with the same carrots and apples, untouched.

Despite his body's need, Joe forced himself to stay upright. His eyes strayed to the front door from time to time. Jim, too, seemed anxious over Beth's continued absence. Between the two of them, they crafted four more crutches until darkness demanded they either stop or light the lantern. Still Beth had not come inside.

Jim's head jerked up and he lunged to his feet.

"What is it?"

Jim didn't answer, he crossed toward the corner of the room where Gerta had reclined and knelt beside the woman.

"Miz Gerta? Miz Gerta?"

Joe watched the man rock the frail form as her name spilled from his lips. Sourness boiled in his belly as the knowledge settled over him. Jim sat back on his heels, head bowed low. He stood up and met Joe's gaze, his face a haggard mask. "She's gone."

―――

The numbness grew and twisted until Beth felt nothing at all. Heard nothing more than the distant squeak of wagons, the whinny of the occasional horse. Riley had come to them in the night with the news that the Confederates were pulling out of Sharpsburg in a long line heading west, over the Potomac. Her heart could not rejoice. He did not stay long enough to discover Gerta's death. No one said a word about the hole Jim had dug in the side yard or the shrouded body of her grandmother, wrapped in the quilt that marked her wedding day. The loss was too fresh, too shocking, yet she should have known. The paleness of Gerta's lips, the obvious discomfort she'd shown. She had not done enough to protect her.

In that same moonless night in which the enemy retreated, Jim carried Gerta's slight form to the grave, lowered her to the ground so he could jump down into the hole, and laid her gently down at his feet. It was Joe who used his mother's Bible to read Scripture. His voice choked with emotion. She could only stare at him as the words of Scripture spilled from his lips. Jim dared to hum a song, low and slow, that Beth did not recognize.

They formed a line and returned to the safety of the cabin. Beth went to the corner where Gerta had slept and tried to make sense of all that had happened, the suddenness. Shouldn't God have warned her somehow? Shouldn't the discovery of her grandmother's death have been more than Jim's ragged voice interrupting her solitude on the porch? The cold chill of the evening air had clutched her harder as Jim's announcement settled around her and was immediately rejected. So she had gone to see for herself. Felt the coldness eating away the natural heat of her grandmother's body when she'd dared to reach out and touch the frail form. And then she had pitched forward, tears demanding release she would not give.

She didn't know how long she had stood there before realizing that Joe's hand had been on her back, her arm. She'd wanted to be left alone, but his hand guided her into a one-armed hug that had further chipped at the wall she'd erected.

"I'm so sorry."

Rage surged back, then ebbed again.

"At least she is in a better place."

Words she'd heard all too often during Leo's funeral as if a silent finger of accusation were being pointed at her.

Huddled on Gerta's bed, she was joined by Joe. He didn't touch her, didn't say a word, but he sat there with his Bible until her vision of him hazed over and she closed her eyes. Sometime in the night she jerked awake. *I love you, Beth.* Gerta's voice went with her from sleep to wakefulness. If only she'd been able to say those words in response to her grandmother's affectionate words. She should have capped her anger more quickly.

She turned her head and wondered why her leg hurt so much when she put weight on it. She leaned to rub her knee and ankle before wandering the few steps to where Jim and Joe slept. She wondered if the Confederates still marched west and strained for sounds of the retreat. Joe, too, might leave. Joe's Bible lay open beside him and, caught beneath his leg, the quilt blocks. Harbingers of God's love. God was her hope, and for the first time in a long time, she knew she needed more than her anger. If Leo's accident was to prove what she was made of, God must have been sadly disappointed to discover her shallowness. She blinked and limped back to the cot Gerta had used. What would she do without her grandmother? And she knew the answer to that lay in their last conversation. Gerta's assertion that God wasn't just her hope for the past, but her future. That by holding on to the past she was rejecting that hope. Gerta had tried to tell her in words. Her mother was trying to show that to her through the quilt pattern. That golden square that beckoned her.

Joe's arm was maimed. How many other soldiers had she seen who had suffered much worse wounds, even died, with God's name on their lips? Begging for a merciful God to take them. And in many cases He would, but some He would not.

Beth buried her face in her hands. They didn't matter though. She knew that deep down. It wasn't a matter of God's intentions toward the sick and dying around her, it was a matter of her heart and her salvation. In the end, she could blame no one but herself because it was her choice what to do with trouble when it spun her world out of control. She'd heard men blame God. Point their finger at the trouble of others and discount God's power because of what they saw as God's failure.

It didn't matter. God didn't need her opinion to run the world, He just needed her to do her part. She bit her lower lip and tried to stifle the sob but it leaked out as God's name whispered from her lips on a rush of air and a flood of salt.

21

Joe woke to an eerie quiet that seemed loud in his ears. It seemed strange when he knew a stream of soldiers like him was marching in a long line through Sharpsburg toward the Potomac and the safety of friendly soil. He was being left behind. The reality was he needed to gather his haversack, slip out into the moonless night and rejoin his regiment.

But Beth had not cried.

Not one tear.

Rage combed the edges of her composure, and while he understood the anger over the death of a loved one, he didn't understand her inability to grieve. It was as if she was frozen inside. He'd seen glimpses of a woman he wanted to know better, but the time and place, his reasons for being with her, were all wrong and he knew it.

He captured one of the crutches Jim had finished for him and pulled to his feet. He wobbled and closed his eyes. He could stay. He knew of men who deserted, sick of the fighting and infrequent rations. Every man he'd talked to dreamed of home as he had known it before the war. Most of his friends joined when they saw those same homes destroyed by the Yanks or heard of a brother or father killed. There was no more strength in him. Stumping down the dirt road and into Sharpsburg would strain the limits of his ability.

His friends would wonder where he'd gotten to. They would want to know about Ben and maybe be able to shed light on the subject. Excuses crumbled beneath the call of duty. Joe retrieved his haversack and lifted it across his shoulder, shifted the crutch to his good arm and took his first, quiet step toward the door. He wanted to say good-bye. To Jim. To Beth. But hesitation was a snag to his determination and he kept his eyes straight forward. At least the old pair of boots would protect his feet, and he, for the moment, would be free from the crawl and bite of body lice.

Union soldiers would pour into Sharpsburg and he would be taken prisoner. He released a pent-up sigh and stroked his hand down the length of his stubbled jaw. He hesitated at the door, turning to see through the dark to the place where Beth would be sleeping. Dimness swallowed her outline. He wanted to see her one more time. Telling her good-bye would ease his guilt for leaving her and his inability to protect her from the ravages of war that she'd been made to endure. Perhaps when the war was over he would come back. Listen for rumors in town and ask questions to make sure she had chased her demons and recaptured her dreams.

"Beth?" he whispered, almost afraid she would answer, in hopes she would sleep and he would be free to leave without further entanglement. Where once she had been strong for him, helped him, he was now stronger and she the weaker. How could he leave her like this? Jim would care for her and make sure she made it back to her parents. The man was faithful and big-hearted. Beth would need someone.

He heard a scraping sound and turned toward the door. Nothing more broke through the stillness, and the tension melted from his shoulders. He knelt beside Beth's still form, aware of nothing more than her breathing and the pale skin of her cheek in the velvet contrast of night.

Gratitude for all she had sacrificed to care for him, for all the others, rose, not to be forgotten or ignored. Her sacrifice was like those made by countless others and he wondered why he felt such allegiance to her. Because he had come to know her. She had shared with him on the horrible journey of his recovery. The night scares. She had sought to soothe him as he had needed to be comforted. And now, in her moment of need, he was leaving?

A hand came down heavy on his shoulder. He gasped and twisted as he rose. A flood of strength bunched his muscles and he cocked his left arm to throw a punch. His wrist was caught in a vise grip.

"No."

"What are you trying to do?" He could barely see Jim's form, his skin tone molding him as one with the darkness. His eyes flashed.

"The Yanks will be on us by morning, if not sooner."

"I need to go."

Jim took a step toward Beth, his words a whisper floating back over his shoulder. "She has lost so much."

He knew what loss was. The wrecking of a land and a way of life by a war that individuals fought more because of the damage they saw to their houses, lands, and loved ones, more than for any politician's ideals.

Jim passed him and ducked through the doorway. Joe followed, closing the door behind him and leaning against it for support.

"If we stay and they capture you . . ."

"I can't desert." He felt the weight of what the man was asking him to do. Afraid to go, reluctant to stay. Returning was his only hope to make sense of what had happened to Ben. His injury would grant him a discharge and he could search for answers from there.

"Her or the war?"

It took him a minute to remember what he'd said before Jim's question. The truth was he couldn't desert her either. She had helped him when he needed it most. Sacrificed for him. And he loved her . . .

"You are too weak to march."

"They'd probably shove me in the back of a medical wagon." And he would bump along, miserable, waiting for a surgeon to tell him it was better for his arm to come off completely. He clenched his right hand, feeling the tendons contract, the muscles move. The numbness had worn off, or maybe it was just a trick of his mind.

"You must work your arm and shoulder in order for it to gain strength."

Lost among thousands of wounded vying for the attention of a doctor or assistant, nurse or volunteer. He would be left to languish as his body continued to knit and heal. Deprived of the soft attention and kindness of Beth . . .

"Help me get her to safety and we'll get you back across the Potomac."

Joe stared hard at the black man. Jim would not beg, and he wanted to care for Beth as she'd cared for him.

The night sounds rolled through his mind, tempting, luring, prodding him to do what was right and honorable. And even as he stood there, Beth's rare smile dangled in his mind like meat to a starving dog.

"We do not have time to waste."

He met Jim's gaze, saw the white of his eyes flash as the man's gaze drifted toward Sharpsburg and the muted sounds of the retreating Rebs. "Then we'd better hurry."

"I can walk," Beth insisted.

"Let Jim carry you. You were limping pretty bad," Joe urged. "We'll make better time."

"You can barely walk yourself."

It was true, but the challenge made him straighten and gulp the air his starved lungs demanded while ignoring the sear of pain radiating from his shoulder, through his back and into his neck. He felt Jim's eyes on him and knew the man also had concerns. If anyone slowed them down it would be him. Part of Joe wondered why the black man had thought it a good idea for him to go with them. He should have thought it through more. He had been manipulated and he knew it. Now. For all Jim's words about him not being able to handle the march, the black man would have known he also wouldn't have been able to traverse the countryside in his weakened state.

"It's not far now," Jim assured. "You and Miss Beth can ride."

He tilted his head to study the man. Jim had something planned. Must have been the fruits of all the black man's ventures out by himself in the last two days.

Joe forced himself to pick up his pace, following the big black man, aware of the way Beth's head bobbed with Jim's every step. She glanced at him over Jim's shoulder and Joe squeezed out a smile.

"Jim. Stop."

The black man whirled with her. She twisted and he finally let her down. Beth came to him, and he wondered if his expression had given away the fire shooting from his shoulder that made it so hard for him to focus enough to place one foot in front of the other.

"He can't go farther." Her hands framed his face. "You're burning up again."

He felt miserable, her hands cool. He didn't want her to ever let go. His arm went around her waist and drew her close. He just needed someone to lean on. She gasped and he was aware of the impropriety of his action but couldn't care.

"Jim?"

The big man took a step closer and crouched as if to lift him. Joe put out a hand, determined to stop the man's action. "I'll be fine."

It was as if Jim didn't hear or the words had never made it past his mind. He was lifted, flung over Jim's shoulder, the blood rushing to his head.

"Someone's coming," Jim's voice held urgency. "Straight ahead."

They bumped along, Jim's steps knifing pain into his shoulder, up his neck, into his head. It was no time to demand to be let down. No time to be weak. He hated it. Needed to be able to walk. Protect Beth and Jim from whatever threat dogged their heels. Instead he felt vague and weak. He missed Beth's cool hands. The solidity of a floor beneath him.

"Jim?" There was a note of surprise in Beth's voice.

"Hurry," Jim urged.

He thought he heard the pound of footsteps, the crush of twigs and leaves. They'd stuck to the woods at Jim's urging. The black man's pace picked up until Joe's pain compounded and squeezed his consciousness to a fine point. Then Jim stopped. He felt himself falling, lifted, lowered to the hard surface of a wagon bed and covered with something. He squinted through the darkness. Heard whispers and didn't recognize a new voice.

Jim's face loomed over him. "Stay quiet and still, Mister Joe. You'll be fine."

He tried to lift his hand, to sit up. Beth's voice whispered against his ear. "Please, Joe. Keep still."

He did then. Rested. With each beat of his heart, the pain lessened and his head cleared. He could see nothing and knew he was in a confined space. He listened hard. Heard a horse's low snuffle.

"They went that way," It was the new voice. "Potomac not far from here. Robbed us of the bread we'd taken in to Sharpsburg for the boys. Thought they was gonna take our horse but they must have heard you coming and skedaddled."

"Strange time for you to be traveling." This voice was formal, refined

"There's another wagon behind us. Coming down from Mercersville with apples and corn, flour, some cider. The women got some quilts together, too."

"What about you?"

"This here is my brother. This here is the woman he works for. They's from Sharpsburg. Been nursing the wounded since the battle up on the mountain."

"She just lost her grandmother." Jim's voice.

He heard a muffled weeping and knew it was Beth. Whether she was acting or not, her timing was impeccable.

The wagon lurched, then began a soft rocking. They were on the road. He closed his eyes and tried to keep still. The heat became unbearable and he longed for the feel of night air against his cheeks.

22

Jim slid Joe from his confines in what seemed like mere minutes later. Night had passed into predawn, the silver light in the east stretching across the sky. Even that dim light made him blink. His head felt cottony. It was hard to think. His whole body ached and he wanted nothing more than to sleep.

"Joe?"

He tried a smile and failed.

"He's burning up. Carry him inside, Jim. Mama will tell you where to put him."

So he was at the home of Beth's parents. It made sense though—Beth's loss, the overwhelming circumstances present in Sharpsburg, and Gerta's death. She would be safe here, as would he. The knot of fear in his belly dissolved and he relaxed as hands and voices became muffled sounds. He was sinking into oblivion and he didn't care.

He woke to soft fingers and the bright light of day. He expected Beth, but saw a version of her twenty-five years into the future.

The woman twisted a cloth and lay it along his forehead. "You must drink as much as possible and eat." She paused and smiled. "I am Anya Bumgartner."

Gray threaded the woman's dark hair. Her soft smile and quiet voice soothed him. She hadn't asked one question of him and he wondered if Beth had told her his true identity or if they would be forced to lie. Looking into the woman's face, he thought it might be best to stick with the truth. She seemed a no-nonsense type woman. Or maybe every mother appeared that way. It brought a rush of warmth to his chest. His mother had been able to read him and his brother every time a lie crossed their lips, resulting in a frown that was at once amused and disappointed. He'd hated that smile because it always poked the lie deeper into his conscience.

"I'm Joe."

"So I've been told."

Already she didn't trust him, though her smile didn't falter. He swallowed. "Where is Beth? Jim?"

"Jim is helping load supplies. Beth is sleeping."

He wanted to ask how she felt about having a Rebel soldier to take care of. Did it disgust her? If her son fought for the Union, surely her feelings would be torn by his presence.

"I should help him."

She tilted her head. "Rest. Get well. Then Jim will help you cross the Potomac."

So she did know.

"I-I'm sorry," he muttered, not understanding his compulsion to apologize.

Her gaze swept over his face, his hair, his arms and chest. "Jim is right. You would not have made the march. It was best for you to stay behind."

He turned his face away. "He should have left me in Sharpsburg."

"They care for you."

He turned his head, and felt the softness of a pillow cradling his head and neck, nuzzling his cheek. The mattress on which he lay was soft, the linens clean and sun-fresh. A wave of despair swept him and he longed for home again, more grieved at the knowledge that the home would be empty. His chest was bare and a fresh bandage had been applied. He plucked at the linen, taut against his skin and considered her words. "I wanted to go back."

"Jim needed you to see Beth to safety. I am grateful for your choice."

He would not argue, though her gratefulness seemed ludicrous in light of the fact he had to be carried most of the way, then hidden the rest of the journey.

"Jim says you are a man of honor. He did not want you to become a prisoner." She shuddered, a light shaking of her shoulders that nevertheless did much to bear out her impression of the prison he most certainly would have been sent to. No doubt she feared not just for him, but for the likelihood of her own son being taken prisoner.

A whisper of movement caught his attention and drew his gaze to Beth. She'd washed her face, pink from the scrubbing, damp tendrils of hair swept back into a neat knot that allowed some of the longer pieces to brush her shoulders.

"Good morning," she said as she limped forward. He saw her fresh dress and the blocks of the quilt in her hand. She spread the blocks on the bed and for a moment, mother and daughter were lost in some unspoken conversation that put a satisfied gleam in Anya's eyes.

"All I could think of was hope," she addressed her mother.

"You see hope now where you saw none before."

Joe didn't know what to make of the conversation and was rescued when Anya rose and nodded toward him. "Take care of Joe while I get breakfast."

"I can help," Beth was quick to reply.

"Rest, Bethie." Anya's hand came down on her shoulder. "Joe needs you."

———∞———

Beth traced the uneven stitches of the quilt blocks she'd joined together over the last few days. Such a whirlwind of events that all led up to losing Gerta. Everything had felt so black and dull just hours before, yet, today, so far from the horrors of war, snug in the safety of the familiar, she felt like the bright spot on the quilt might not be so far away any more. God was as close as her prayers.

And then there was Joe. She raised her gaze to his and felt the weight of her mother's parting words; *Joe needs you.* His fever had risen. He remained weak, but under the watchful gaze of his green eyes, something else demanded attention. He was telling her something. The press of his hand on hers and the tangle of their fingers.

She broke her gaze and glanced out the window. He was only a man whom Jim revered because of his compassion toward the blacks whose lives he had saved. It wouldn't have bothered her one way or the other if he had traipsed along after the retreating Rebs. But even as the words rolled through her mind she knew they weren't true. Joe was more than a Rebel. He'd been a refuge to her during the height of the battle. He had shared in the worry and fear and he had been there in the darkest of night.

"You must feel better."

"I do." His drawl seemed more pronounced, less hateful than those first days when his few words were weighted with the reminder that she was working over the enemy. She withdrew her hand as the blush crept into her cheeks.

She reached to spread the quilt blocks and wondered if she would ever find the heart to finish the quilt. Those five blocks, bound together in the darkest of days, encapsulated the roll of every emotion and feeling she'd experienced in the last week. They were her symbol of victory.

"I'll have to go back, Beth. They need all the help they can get."

If she dreaded anything, it was this moment. On one hand, she understood. He was a soldier and the South was in retreat. His life in the North would be no life at all. A prisoner. And the likelihood of him dying in those prisons was high.

When she met his steady gaze, there was no remorse, just the thrust of determination in his jaw. All that she had felt for him, the closeness, swirled away in that moment. Her anger elbowed aside reason.

"And there's Meredith. She must miss you terribly."

Joe's brows lowered. "Meredith?" His lips compressed as his gaze shifted to a point over her shoulder. "She won't want me either."

She absorbed his words. *Either.* Anger turned to something else entirely. "You're a man anyone would love. You're getting stronger."

Something flickered in his expression before she dropped her gaze to her lap.

"It won't matter to her. She wants a whole man."

She raised her face, a new awareness pulsing through her . . . "She doesn't love you?"

"I thought she did. I wanted her to love me." He went silent for a stretch and Beth let him gather his thoughts.

Those very words were on the tip of her tongue. *I love you, Joe,* was backed up by the pounding of her heart. She half hoped it did not reflect in her eyes. Not yet. Just because he didn't think Meredith loved him didn't mean he didn't felt anything for her.

"Will you read to me, Beth?"

In the bright light of day, he could read to himself, but having him near was comforting and she wanted to keep an eye on him. To make sure he ate and worked his weak hand as Jim had told her he had encouraged Joe to do.

She lifted her face to the warmth of the sun spilling through the glass, unmarred by the battle. She pressed her hand to the wavy crystal surface and felt the heat on her palm. "If not for Meredith, then why do you need to go back?"

"I have to find out what happened to Ben."

"They won't—" She bit her tongue on what she'd been about to say.

"I'll get discharged. It'll free me to find out what happened to my brother."

Her heart seemed to wilt in her chest. "You're so sure you'll be able to do that?"

"I don't know but I have to try. His death doesn't make sense and . . ."

"Ben would want you to move on."

She turned from the sunshine and he was watching her. He stretched his hand out to her. She hesitated before pressing her palm against his. "I want to move on but I need to know what happened. It was so strange. He was there and then he wasn't . . ." Squeezing his fingers brought his attention back to her. "I'll come back to you, Beth."

Her breath caught. She saw him swallow.

"Do you want that too?"

Whatever lay between them, she knew she wanted to give it a chance, and the only way to do that was for her to say yes. Did he realize she wasn't whole? It was the secret she had managed to avoid revealing—because he was also at a disadvantage, unable to see her awkwardness from the perspective of a man on his feet.

"I'm not . . ."

"Bethie?"

"My limp. I'm not what you think, Joe."

"I don't understand."

"My limp. It's permanent."

He was so quiet and she feared staring into his eyes now. Rejection. He would recoil from the idea of courting a cripple as Riley had.

"It's not just . . . I always limp. My ankle was damaged when I tried to rescue Leo."

"Look at me, Beth."

She didn't want to. Tears balanced on her lashes. He tugged on her hand and she finally relented. His expression was not one of horror or disgust, and he didn't withdraw his hand but tightened his grip on hers.

"You said you didn't reach him in time . . ."

"It was more than that. I was on my way out and . . ." She could smell the smoke again. The horror of the flames and the burn of her lungs from heat and smoke all came back to her. Drawing deep breaths, she tried to force back the panic. The fear. The sound of Leo's cries reverberated in her head all over again. She knew the moment she wouldn't be able to reach Leo. His cries became whimpers. She couldn't see anything, eyes streaming from the burn of the thick, acrid smoke. She'd felt the rush of cool air on her face. Flames roared higher behind her and the ominous creak over her head. Pushing forward, she had touched heat and then the crack and twist of what she now knew had been the beam over her head collapsing. Pinning her.

Joe released her hand and she felt again the cold chill of knowing she would die, pinned beneath the massive weight.

S. Dionne Moore

Joe pulled her close and she relaxed into the warmth of his embrace. His whispers against her hair, near her ear, reassuring her that she would be fine.

"It's all done, Bethie. It's all over."

Pillowing her head against his shoulder, she let his words eat away the terror. "I wanted so much to get to him."

"You were brave to try."

"It wasn't enough."

He pulled back and touched the wetness on her cheeks. "Leo wouldn't come back if he could. He's enjoying heaven too much." He touched her chin and tilted her face to meet his eyes. "Seems we both have to work on moving on."

But he hadn't seen how badly she limped every day, hard work or no. Or how easy it was for her to fall. What man wanted a wife who was twisted and ungraceful?

"My mother used to say God brings people to us to show us new ways of old thinking."

Is that what this was? Joe was showing her new ways of old thinking? He was challenging her not with his words, but by stirring emotions she thought herself incapable of feeling and, really, worked hard not to feel at all.

"I'm so sorry about your grandmother."

She flinched at the mention of Gerta. The quagmire of loss sucked at her anew. But Gerta had died doing what she felt was important and that made all the difference. Still, the knowledge didn't dull the ache of loss for any of them. "I can't believe she's gone."

"We'll go back when things have settled and give her a proper burial."

She wiped at her eyes and nestled her hand into his as his statement settled into her mind, and the easy way he used the word "we."

23

Determination had oozed from Ben in the weeks following Sue's wake. He had been a different man and a much more intense brother. Consumed with a need for revenge against the collective forces stirring the country to war that resulted in Sue's death. At the time, Joe had watched his brother's fervor, not quite understanding the basis for it, but he'd followed along thinking it best they stick together. In battle at Malvern Hill, they had received word of their mother's death but were denied a pass to return home.

Every battle seemed to further goad Ben. He grew restless, often wandering in the night when they bivouacked. Soldiers of rank appeared to Ben in the darkness. Ben never introduced them but always wandered off to speak to his visitor in low tones. Joe had thought nothing of it at the time. Now, a chilling accusation simmered. Had his brother become a spy for the Union?

Joe's throat thickened. He'd dreamed of Ben and that final night when the shot rang out and took his brother's life. Dying on the battlefield was an easy explanation, but to be shot by a man who might or might not have been the enemy, while the shooter left him to live . . .

He made a fist with his left hand and held it up. Tendons and veins lined the back of his hand. His arm thinner than usual. Anger at his injuries, at the senseless death of his brother and sister and mother. But as quick as the emotion flared hot, it cooled. There was no one to blame. Everyone suffered. The only option was to look forward to a time when the war would end and things would return to what would have to be a new pattern of life.

He would be alone as he had never been before.

Stroking his bristled jaw, he contemplated the hollowness of his existence. Beth hadn't committed to him. She thought her limp must make a difference somehow, but it didn't. Knowing her had helped him realize how weak of character Meredith was. The two women were like summer and winter.

He wanted to stay here. To be with Beth and pursue wherever their relationship would lead, but it was unconscionable for him to stay in the North when he would be hated and shunned. He could not assume that her parents would approve any relationship and even if they did there would be no rest for him until he could grasp the reason Ben was shot.

If he could find out nothing, and indeed, he might not be able to, then he would have to satisfy himself that he had tried; but not trying at all wasn't an option.

Would Beth wait for him? Would he return to the North to endure being the hated enemy, shunned because of the allegiance he had for his home. Or would she agree to follow him to the South?

He didn't know. There were no answers and he had to trust. No greater one to trust than God. He only wished he had his mother's Bible, which Beth would return to read to him from later. A smile curved his lips and he shut his eyes. When all else failed, he could pray.

Her father spread his arms wide upon catching sight of her. She needed no greeting beyond that and went to him, overjoyed at the feeling of security his presence offered. "Grandmama . . ." Her voice muffled into his shoulder. He stroked her hair once, then held her at arm's length.

"Jim told me all about it." His eyes misted. "She always was the stubborn one."

It was the harshest thing she'd ever heard her father say against his mother.

"But she was a hard worker and would walk a mile to help someone in need."

She pressed her fingers to her lips to hold back the grip of a sob.

"Come, daughter, there is much that needs to be done, and Gerta would want us to offer what help we can give."

"I was there, father. I saw it all."

His face gentled. "Yes, Jim said as much. He told me how brave you were." He started toward the house motioning her to follow. "And you've brought a soldier home."

Words stuck in her throat. "A Confederate soldier."

Nicklaus Bumgartner sent her a sideways glance. "Who risked his life to save slaves. Sounds like a man with morals, Southern or not."

Tension ebbed from her shoulders and neck.

"Do you still want to pursue nursing?"

Strange that he would ask. Surely he must know how desperately she was needed now on the battlefields. Everyone was needed. But deep down inside, she was exhausted. The tension leading up to the battle outside their town had drained her in a way she'd never expected and only now, removed from the fray, could she see what a toll it had taken. And then Gerta's unexpected death . . .

"I think not, but what is there for me to do?"

"You could teach."

"You've given this some thought," she rubbed at her leg, sending him a small smile.

Nicklaus stopped and so did Beth. "We are preparing to go out and offer our help to those who need it. You have endured enough and your mother will need your help here with chores. And there's your leg to consider."

"I'm fine."

"No," he reached to squeeze her shoulder. "You're not. Your limp is worse and there is an exhaustion in your eyes that does much to tell me what you've endured."

"God has helped me."

She didn't miss the relief that eased the lines bracketing his eyes. Moisture collected in the corners of his eyes.

"We had hoped you would finally come to see the distance you had put between yourself and God."

"Mother sent the blocks . . ."

"We both saw the change in you, in your spirit. She had worked over them in hopes you would understand." Nicklaus let his hand fall away. "Perhaps the Lord is leading you in a different way now, daughter. Something he has yet to reveal." He stared off into the distance, at the clouds scudding across the sky, then back to her. "There is affection between you and this soldier."

A protest rose to her lips but she could not speak it. "I—"

Nicklaus chuckled. "Jim is discreet but he is observant as well. It is a quality I admire in him."

She stared at the tips of her shoes. "He's a Rebel," she whispered.

"He is flesh and blood, heart and soul."

When she found the courage to meet her father's steady gray gaze, she knew he spoke from the heart and would welcome Joe into their family. A hot blush crept up her neck at the thought. For despite everything, Joe was not hers to claim. And once he saw how ungraceful she truly was, his mind would turn his heart against her.

24

Her mother's cheeks were reddened from the heat of the oven in the summer kitchen. A slender black woman came in on Anya's heels, her face creasing into a shy, fleeting smile. The door that had just slapped closed behind the black woman, yawned open again and a black man, arms full of garden produce, entered. The woman began taking things from the man's arms. Sweet potatoes, onions. It was a replay of Gerta's return from the garden that morning less than a week ago. Fleeting memories that would be cherished in the wake of her sudden death.

Her mother nodded to the pair. "Pearl and Roy. They're the ones who helped bring you all home." She addressed Pearl. "Did you get your father settled?"

"Yes, ma'am."

There was a lilt to Pearl's voice that identified her as Southern. She recalled that voice now. The same accent she heard from Joe. A deeper connection was made. "You're the ones who brought Joe to us."

Pearl glanced at Roy. The man nodded. "Jim told us to come here."

Roy's accent was the same as Joe's, soft, Southern. "You risked your lives for us last night."

Pearl and Roy shared a look, the woman continuing to help relieve the man of the produce. Anya stepped closer, a joyous smile lit her features. "They wanted to help. We were worried when the battle was raging so close." Her smile wilted into sadness. "Gerta has not been well for many years. Her heart."

"You should have seen her, Mama."

"I have seen her at work. She loves—loved—what she did." Anya turned and plucked down an apron for Beth. "We will work as we talk. We have much to do before the wagons arrive."

All along, during the long days and nights, her mother and father had been helping the very slaves who had brought Joe to Gerta. "I worked on the quilt blocks."

Anya raised a long knife and sliced a sweet potato in half, then quarters, as if she hadn't heard. Beth took the pieces and cut them even smaller as Pearl kneaded a trough of dough, sprinkling flour as she worked.

"You put several together," Anya wiped at a strand of hair with the back of her hand, moving back in time for Roy to place more washed sweet potatoes in front of her.

Despite being in the comfort of her childhood home, close to her mother and father and out of the way of danger, Beth could still taste the terror. "It was a welcome respite from . . ." She wondered if she would ever be able to shake the horror.

Her mother laid her knife aside, put her hand beneath Beth's arm, and directed them outside into the warm air. Her mother let go and pushed Beth gently onto a chair, then sat beside her.

"You have experienced much more than most."

She lifted her face to the beams of light. "You didn't want me to be a nurse."

"No," Anya's voice was firm. "No, Bethie, it wasn't that at all."

For the first time, she thought she understood. "It was spiritual."

Relief smoothed the wrinkles of her mother's expression. "Now you see."

"I knew the quilt was your way of showing me something."

"I had hoped you would seek comfort in it. I chose the colors to show you that your limp and Leo's death did not have to be a darkness that forever shaped your soul."

Beth sank to her knees and laid her head in her mother's lap. "It was what I saw when I looked at it. Joe, too. The colors, the message . . ."

"It is an old pattern. Goose Chase. It reminded me of you. Your father and I saw the darkness that was trying to consume you."

She squeezed her eyes shut as Anya's fingers smoothed the hair above Beth's ear. "It brought me home again." She wondered if her mother would understand what she meant. Not the physical home, but the spiritual. When she lifted her head, Anya's eyes were full. She leaned into her mother's arms.

"I am so happy."

"Thank you, Mama."

They worked elbow-to-elbow shaping bread, making pies, packing jars of pickled pig's feet, preserves, boiled eggs, and potatoes already baked and left to cool. Women from around town gathered at the church down the road to rip linens into bandages and donate blankets, clothes, shoes, whatever could be spared. Hogs were slaughtered and sausage making begun in earnest, not for their private stores, but to help support the thousands of wounded flooding Sharpsburg, Boonsboro, Reisterstown, and others overwhelmed with the sick and dying.

Beth escaped to check on Joe who slept through most of the excitement. She let him sleep, contenting herself with watching the quiet rise and fall of his chest. Gratified to know that answers might await him in the form of Pearl and Roy. It would be Joe's chance to learn the truth of what happened that night, instead of living with the fragments his traumatized mind served up in splinters.

Beneath the window she watched the new wave of women arrive, their sons or daughters doing the driving as the women tried to keep their youngsters in check. Beth drank in the willingness of the townsfolk to help. They asked her about the battle, slack-jawed at the stories she told of the dead and wounded in the fields surrounding Sharpsburg. Smells of death. Of Teresa Kretzer's flag and the noise of the Confederate retreat. She knew nothing more firsthand, but was gratified to see the way her stories sparked a caring and renewed dedication in the women toward helping those South of them.

She noted that Pearl said little, that Roy never said anything, and that he stayed close to her father in the buildings surrounding the farmhouse, always busy loading something more into the bed of an already full wagon. She knew that the reason for the man's silence extended beyond working hard. She wondered if the very women who flocked to hear the stories of the battle would gasp in horror and brand the Bumgartners as traitors if they knew a Rebel soldier lingered in a spare bedroom upstairs, or that Pearl and Roy, and Roy's father Jonah, were all from the Deep South, escaped slaves that had found a home with her mother and father.

With every wave of women, her stories had to be retold. Until, finally, the telling had chipped at her and she sought out

Joe as she had sought him out during the dark days. He slept, and as he did she nestled her hand beneath his and lowered her head to her arms.

∞∞∞

Joe blinked awake feeling like a great bear waking after a long winter. The thought brought a smile. The pain in his shoulder wrestled him back to reality and twisted his lips into a grimace. There was something else, too. A subtle vibration that had woken him.

He cracked open an eye and saw a black woman at his side. She was smoothing a cool cloth over his warm skin. Every time she leaned forward, the bed wiggled.

When she saw him watching her, she lowered her eyes and let the rag she'd been using fall back into the basin of water. "I am Pearl."

She did not turn and scurry away as so many blacks did in the South in the presence of a white man. Except Lela. The housemaid who had cared for him, Ben, and Sue in their youth, seldom backed down to any man or woman, white, black or otherwise. He'd loved Lela.

He licked his lips. "Could I have a drink?"

She raised her gaze to his. "I'll get you one."

"And Beth—I mean M—"

"I'll fetch her for you."

Her voice nudged him. It was more than the obvious southern drawl. It was familiar. When Pearl returned with water, he drank long and deep. Muscles bunched from disuse. A soreness that registered through his back and sides. Stretching upward, he wiggled himself to a sitting position needing to work the stiffness from his muscles. Pearl took a step back,

174

grabbed up a shirt, and handed it to him without saying a word. He squinted at her. "I know you."

She returned his stare, saying nothing.

Her smooth skin glowed. Her head, wrapped in a kerchief, barred him from seeing her hair to determine her age. Thirties would be his best guess. Southern . . . a V appeared between his eyes as he tried to combine the voice with the face. And then it came to him. He used the footboard to get to his feet, the surprise coursing through him.

"Ben. You were the ones we rescued." His world tilted. Spun. He hung on.

"We're forever thankful for your sacrifice." Her gaze went to her feet. "For your brother's kindness to us."

"Tell me what happened."

She passed him the tin of water.

He ignored it.

"You found us in that rundown—"

He waved his hand impatiently. "No. Ben. My brother was shot. What do you remember?"

Pearl shrank back, sensitive to the forcefulness in his voice.

He stuffed back his anxiousness. He reached for the tin of water and gulped it down, passing it back to her with a smile he did not feel. "Please."

She stared at her feet. "He rose up out of nowhere. Your brother was helping you along the way as fast as he dared to go, aiming us toward Maryland. We was almost there when that man rose up in front of us. He had no eyes for us, just your brother."

Her words stirred the memories. He remembered falling. A sudden thrust away from Ben's side.

"Shoved you away from him and went to swing his rifle around, but the man raised his and fired before your brother had a chance. He crumpled to the ground. Ray tried to carry him, but your brother was bleeding too much . . . he was dead. You were all we had left and you'd already told us the direction we needed to take. We vowed we'd get ourselves North, then find you some help. Roy asked around for a woman who might be kind to a Rebel and we waited 'til midnight to go to the woman's house. She fed us. Told us to go to Jim."

His anger rose hot, hotter than the fever that raged off and on. He didn't want the general story, he wanted specifics. His rage gave him strength and he took a step closer to her. "You must know who shot him."

She shrank away from him, her eyes wide.

He stilled and tried to rein in his emotion. "A description." But it had been dark. Even his image was vague, the mismatched uniform his only clear clue and he often wondered if that had been a product of his dreams. "Sounds. The time or place. Did Ben say anything?" Hadn't he heard Ben's voice utter something in his dreams?

"Please, sir!"

Her shriek pulled him back to what he was doing. His hand on her wrist. His grip tight. He released her immediately and retreated.

She burst into tears and his anger blew away like chaff on the wind. He stared at his left hand as if its grip had betrayed him. Pearl slid away from him and bolted out the door just as Beth entered the room, confusion knitting her brows.

"Joe?"

He half-turned. "I scared her." Truth be told, he'd scared himself.

"They're the ones who brought you to us that night. Her and—"

"I know," he turned his back to her, gaze landing on the overflowing wagon and the women and men working hard to fill another wagon. More people arrived by the minute. The temptation to go down there and reveal his identity rubbed at him.

He heard her take a step closer, her skirts swishing as she moved. Her hand on his arm. "Perhaps you should lie down again. I'll bring you something to eat."

He faced her. Her expression glowed. She was home. Happy and whole. And he was miles away.

Her expression softened and a smile lit her face and set her eyes to dancing. "I think my mother has a pie for you."

He drank in the high color of her cheeks, the smooth gloss of her hair, the strand that fluttered around the corner of her left eye. Her smile faded and he wondered if her heart beat as hard as his, or if she understood that she was all he had that was comfortable and familiar.

His left hand gripped the post, then slipped out to rest at her waist. When he leaned forward, she didn't gasp in horror or step away, which he took as a good sign. She met his kiss with a gasp that melted to surprise. She allowed her lips to linger on his, took a tiny step closer. She broke the kiss as she stepped back, her expression both amazed and horrified. Her fingers stroked the place where his lips had just lingered. His heart beat like the drone of men marching hard toward the next battle.

"Beth . . ." her name slipped from his lips and he knew not what he was asking or why he had kissed her. It meant something, a kiss, but he only knew she had been there and he had needed comfort. A sign. Affirmation. But he would not apologize.

⁂

Beth felt bruised by the kiss. She had allowed him a liberty she should not have, while enjoying the unexpected attention much more than she should. The two points warred within her. She should slap him, but her response had been a choke-hold. Her mind told her it was too soon for love. Once he saw her on a daily basis, her limp, whatever affection he held for her would fade.

They stared at each other for a languorous minute, breathless with the shock of the moment, or the depth of the response the contact stirred. She was his nurse. He had been her support of sorts. A friend.

Nothing more.

The milling of people outside the window penetrated the silence of the moment. She still could not look away from his penetrating gaze. No rebuke formed on her lips and she wondered if this would be the first and only chance she would ever have of being kissed. She took a bold step forward. He met her with a hand to her waist, swayed slightly toward her as she rose on tiptoe to taste of his lips again. Maybe he would love her . . .

His hand circled to the middle of her back though he held her away from him, eyes searching hers. "I've got to leave."

She didn't want to hear it. Not while her heart was soaring on the gossamer wings of a new hope.

He lowered his face to hers, his arm urging her closer. Salt added to the taste of the moment and she didn't know whether the tears were hers or his or both. She lifted her hand to his face and touched wetness. She pulled back as a sob swelled and choked. Her throat clutched for air and she swiped hard at the tears on her cheeks as his words chanted through her mind. She would soon be alone again.

25

He swallowed hard, bereft of her warmth, dizzy. He gripped the banister and sank to the bed, watching Beth. Everything in him wanted to drown out the crazy world and the infernal war and continue this moment forever. But it wasn't right and they would both regret giving in to whatever was drawing them together.

Leaving would mean finding answers about Ben. Locating his body and taking it back down South to rest next to his mother and father. He could at least do that. He could rejoin his regiment in some capacity that didn't require shooting a gun or marching for long distances. Supply wagons needed drivers. But rejoining the fray meant pitting himself against Beth's North. Somehow claiming sides seemed trivial in the face of what they shared. Though he was not foolish enough to think all would share his view.

"I'll write to you."

She hugged herself, nodding, not meeting his gaze.

Her silence was killing him. "Beth, say something."

"There is nothing to say. You must do what you think is best."

He closed his eyes and massaged his head. Even now he still would not have the strength to travel far. They might still have a few weeks before the fever stopped draining the little strength he did have.

Her shoulders squared and her chin came up.

"We have time, Beth." He didn't know if he said it for himself or for her, only that he hated the awkwardness of what he had set into motion. "Maybe weeks."

"There are men out there who need our help. My help. You expect me to be here by your side as they suffer?"

"Then maybe I should leave now." He flung the words at her.

Her gaze stabbed at him. "If that's what you want."

———

Beth's mother waited for her at the bottom of the steps. Flour smeared along the backs of her hands and a smudge marred her soft cheek. "Is all well, daughter?"

What could she answer?

Anya's worry ran deeper, Beth knew, but her mother was and always had been a woman of few words. "Jim has offered to take him across the Potomac so he will avoid being taken prisoner."

She shuddered at the thought of Joe hauled off to a Union prison.

Her mother wiped her hands down her apron, face angled back toward the kitchen and the women who came and went in and out of the house. "Make sure he is fed well and he'll gain his strength quickly."

"If the fever would just go away."

Her attention returned to Beth. "It will. Give it time. Give *him* time."

She glanced hard at her mother, wondering at the emphasis of the statement, but Anya was heading back toward the kitchen, out of earshot.

By nightfall, the wagons were packed and ready. The men would drive them into Sharpsburg in the morning. She had volunteered to return, but her moment of bravery melted as the grandfather clock ticked toward midnight. Every horror she'd witnessed beat at her. Too easily, she could recall the unreality of going about a normal routine while surrounded by the groans of men mauled by an enemy to whom they could not put a name. She felt, again, the stretch of nerves they labored under for those three days leading up to Wednesday. Again and again she recalled those moments in the cellar when all three of them had huddled with Joe as the dying soldiers' breaths became more and more labored, more ragged. The shells raining down with no thought for the damage they had already incurred or the men who twitched or screamed at the familiar sounds that had already claimed legs or arms or sanity.

She sighed and swept back the light blanket knowing sleep would not come while her mind spun. Sitting up, she let her feet touch the floor, swung them back and forth, returning, for an instant, to the childlike innocence of measuring the distance of her feet to the floor. She sprang up as the image dissolved and shrugged into her dressing gown.

Her hand had just clasped the doorknob when a board outside her door released a groan. Someone was moving down the hall. Panic gripped her. *Joe.* It had to be him packing up in preparation of leaving. He had seemed so determined. She had sent Jim to care for him after their kiss, unable to face him or the result of the cross words she'd spoken.

When she stepped into the hallway, she saw that the broad back at the head of the steps was too wide to be Joe's.

"Jim."

The black man glanced over his shoulder at her, but kept moving. She followed, determined to know whether Joe had made plans. If his fever still raged. If Jim judged Joe strong enough to cross the Potomac on his own . . .

At the landing, she stepped into the circle of light that encompassed Jim and was surprised to see her mother and father.

"It is late, daughter," her father admonished.

"Shouldn't you be to bed as well?"

"Your mother was worried."

"You said yourself you couldn't sleep either," Anya protested.

Her father's soft chuckle was his admission. "Sit and join us, Bethie"

She turned to Jim. "How is Joe?"

The black man sagged onto a bench. "When I took him food, he picked at it. I told him he should eat and he tried . . ."

"Jim came to get me," her mother inserted. "His fever is back. I checked the wound and replaced the bandage but I fear there is something deep inside him that is causing the redness. Doctor Bradley is a risk."

She knew it to be true. The Mercersville doctor had no use for anyone with secesher sympathies.

"What about . . ."

"They've all headed south to aid our army. I've done what I could. Pearl helped me open the wound and clean it out. All we can do now is pray."

"But he was so much better this afternoon."

"The conditions under which you and Gerta worked were less than ideal and her eyes were old. You can't blame yourself, daughter."

She wondered, then, if Pearl had told her mother of her encounter with Joe.

"He seems bent on leaving to find his brother."

"Ben is dead," she said, her voice flat.

"Oh."

She didn't miss the anxious glance her mother sent her father, no doubt sharing her distress over the thought of Jedidiah dying. "Have you . . . heard word from Jed?"

"He is well. He hopes to slip away to see us but they are busy burying those that fell and he doubts he will be able to come."

Her heart rose with the news. Jedidiah. In Sharpsburg. Walking, talking, *alive.*

"His message confirms that it is the nightmare you expressed."

She shuddered and pulled the edges of her wrapper tighter. Jim rose and slipped out the back door leaving them alone as a family. Her father and mother shared a look she could not interpret.

"If Jed returns, it could be a problem, Bethie."

Her father let the statement dangle. Her knees went weak as the meaning dawned and she slipped onto the last empty chair in the room. "Joe."

"Jim seems to think he means something to you. He says Gerta saw it, too."

"Saw what?"

Her father fidgeted. "A bond. Something more than that of a woman caring for a sick man."

She wanted to laugh. To dismiss the statement as absurd. Her, a cripple, loving a man? She'd loved Riley and he had turned his back on her. Beth's attempt at dismissing her mother's words sounded more like a strangled groan than a laugh. Was this the reason Gerta and Jim had brought Joe along? Despite him being the enemy. The kiss had changed everything.

Unexpected though it was, she couldn't deny the emotion it had stirred. All the feelings she thought herself incapable of, dead to, had surged to the forefront. For a moment, too, she had hoped for something more than the menial existence the injury had left her. And then Joe had talked of his need to leave . . .

When she focused on her mother and father, they were sharing a long look. She would have to let Joe go. She had no choice.

"You must stay here with him," her father stated. "I don't want you back in Sharpsburg, or Boonsboro. Not now. Stay here. See Joe back to health."

"He's leaving."

Anya frowned. "Not in the condition he's in now."

It was her turn to frown. He would grow restless again. She'd seen it before in his unconsciousness and it would be there again. While she could understand his need to discover what had happened to his brother, she didn't understand why he had to leave to do that. He could stay and make a vow. But he would have to have a reason to do so, and Joe had never expressed love for her.

"If he must go, it is for the best," her father said. The words hit her hard. On one hand, they acknowledged she might have feelings for him, on the other they agreed that he should return to the South.

"I need to do my duty to the others."

Her mother rose and came toward her. Anya's face showed love and concern, enough to twist Beth's heart. Her mother's hands framed her face and her earnest eyes demanded her full attention. "You have done your duty. Rest, daughter. Your father is right. Stay here. Protect Joe. Heal whatever it is that troubles you."

There it was again, the assertion that she was troubled.

"Follow the path of the quilt. God will lead you."

She couldn't grasp what her mother was telling her. It was as if her mother had forgotten their earlier conversation. "I am following God, Mama."

"Then let Him heal."

26

H*eal.* Such a bitter word for her. To heal meant to forget. To forgive. Yet the wound of her youth would never go away. She would always be scarred by the accident and the rejection.

For the second time in the night, she sat up. She stretched her leg, flexed her foot to work the kinks out of the muscles before she stood. The sun would stretch over the horizon at any moment and she wanted to check on Joe. If her parents thought it best for her to stay, she would do so, but heal?

She worked the buttons of her pristine blouse, thankful for clothes that weren't stained by the blood and gore of dying soldiers. She shuddered at the memory.

Joe slept soundly, Pearl at his side sponging the heat from his skin. Shame washed over her at leaving Joe because of an unexpected kiss and at their exchange of barbs. She touched her lips and nodded at Pearl that she would take over his care.

"He's not taken anything, Miss."

What little weight he had gained would continue to melt away if fever refused to relinquish its grip. At least he didn't thrash about, but when she touched his forehead, heat rose from it like a sunburn.

She continued to sponge his skin, his arms, but every stroke against his hot skin evaporated the water. "Pearl?" She turned to see if the woman had left yet.

"Ma'am?"

"Would you send Jim up when you see him?" She took note of Pearl's wan expression. "And you sleep. I'll help Mama as much as possible today."

"Thank you."

She finished working on the wound, sponging away fresh blood from the latest surgery then rewrapping the site. Leaning back, she rolled her head to release tightness and picked up the folded quilt blocks and slipped out the needle. There would certainly be plenty of time for her to add another block. She smoothed the material and joined together the seams trying to block out the play of colors. The draw of the bright central square. God. She'd given God her heart. What more could He want? Let Him heal . . . Heal what?

Her needle dipped into the seam and she began, the rhythm soothing. She leaned toward the basin of cool water. Dabs of the cloth against his skin seemed to do so little. What if he died? Infection was setting in. The thought stabbed fear, yet it was the only reason for the fever to rage so high. She trusted her mother's care, just as she trusted Gerta's.

Lord . . . ?

A lone tear rolled down her cheek and perched on the edge of her lip. She tasted its salt as she raised the cloth and stroked down Joe's arm to the tips of his fingers. She'd clung to his presence during the battle. He had freely offered her the comfort of his presence. Not drawing back even though he knew she was crippled. Then why was he leaving? His brother was dead. What did the details of his death matter now? It must be Meredith . . . Despite his words he must care for her.

She ran the cloth over each of the fingers on his right hand, bending each one as she worked. She lifted his forearm and bent it toward his upper arm. She had no idea if it helped or not, but it seemed the right thing to do. When she lifted her eyes, he was watching her. She started. Warmth crept up her neck and into her cheeks.

"I thought it might help."

His eyes were glazed with the heat. He closed them and she turned her attention to sponging his face.

A sigh slipped from him when the cool cloth touched his neck. His eyes fluttered open. She labored over the other side of his face, his left arm, all the while feeling his gaze on her. She wondered what he was thinking, feeling. If his shoulder hurt . . . if he remembered their kiss . . .

She dipped water into a mug for him and lifted his head for him to drink. He sipped and turned his head away.

"You have to take more, Joe."

The green of his eyes was blurred by the fever. She put her hand against his cheek, his forehead, torturing herself with the possibility that the fever could take him.

His lips moved.

"Sh." She pressed her finger to his mouth.

His eyes closed and she turned her head away, grateful that he would not witness her shattering. She had already cried so much, but it never seemed enough, it never seemed to touch the spot in her heart. She would forever be grateful to Joe for the kiss. If nothing else, she would have that of him to savor.

"Beth . . ."

She ran her sleeve across her eyes and pasted on a smile.

"Don't cry."

"It's what we women do best."

He licked his lips and she waved the cup of water at him. "Drink as much as you can," she admonished as she lifted his head and held the cup to his lips. It wasn't much but she had no choice but to be satisfied that it was something.

"Read."

She sat down and picked up the Bible, the pages opened to Hebrews, chapter 6. The first verse left her lips, uncomprehending of the message. She read it again, the mention of dead works and faith toward God pounding her conscience. Clearing her throat, she stole a glance at Joe. His eyes were closed. She continued, the sharp prick stabbing harder as she read verses four, then five, and finally six.

She, the most humbled person, by a cruelty that had left her maimed for life. Who could be more humbled by such a senseless act?

Shutting the Bible, she set it aside. Joe never stirred. She picked up the quilt blocks and sunk her needle through the seam she'd started, counting the stitches to amuse herself. Humming broken verses of hymns, even daring a verse of "Dixie." Anything to keep her mind occupied.

His name was repeated, over and over, until his muscles ached from running, stopping, turning. He couldn't find the person who called to him. It was a soft voice. Feminine. His sister, but not his sister. His mother . . .

He lifted his head to catch the soft sound. She was there. Waiting for him. Clutching something in her hands. The quilt. Beth . . .

It was important. The quilt. The message. She was hurting, and even as he watched, her smile faded and she leaned to touch her leg, her foot. And then, she was gone and he was strangling against the blackness.

His body convulsed and his eyes snapped open. His breathing was heavy. A shadow rose up from beside him and he tensed, unsure why his arms felt so heavy, his legs so weak.

"Bad nightmare. It's a good thing you woke up. I thought you might start yelling all over again."

Little by little, he relaxed, chilled by the cool air against his skin and the petite presence of the black woman. Pearl, he remembered. He'd scared her earlier and needed to apologize. She knew something about Ben. Later. He would ask her about it again later.

"Let's get you cleaned up. That fever be draining you of everything."

He blinked dumbly at the chair Pearl had been sitting in, wanting to see Beth there. Hear her voice as he had in the dream. Why had she disappeared so suddenly? Panic stuttered the beat of his heart even as he felt the dampness of his own sweat in which he lay. Was Beth dead too?

"Beth."

Pearl wrung the cloth between her capable hands and began patting down his face. "She sleeping."

She was safe. Asleep. Joe closed his eyes, absorbing the coolness of the cloth.

"If'n you're feeling strong enough, I'll shave you."

He wanted to protest, but already she had the brush, whipping it around, dabbing at his face.

"You'll feel better with these whiskers off."

Obediently, he lifted his chin as she raked the straight edge down his throat. He angled his face toward her, then away, according to the place she was shaving. She dabbed at his face with a warm towel, followed by the cool water.

"Much better."

Despite the weakness, he did feel better for the shaving.

"We'll change those sheets now. Been too long already, but you having that fever made us too worried to do much more than keep your skin cool and make you drink."

His fever had broke? He still felt hot. "How long?"

"Fever been raging for about four days. You been in and out the whole time. Plumb wore Miss Beth down to a nub, which is why I sent her off to bed."

She worked as she spoke, helping him roll to one side, then the other as she stripped the linen from the bed and put down a clean sheet. She helped him into a clean pair of long underwear that he'd never seen before but couldn't find the strength to question. Every movement required more than he had to give. He released a grateful sigh when Pearl finally pulled the light blanket back up to his chest and bid him to sleep, her hand to his head.

"Think the worst is over. You sleep. Miss Beth should be here when you wake."

He didn't want to sleep but the little bit of effort required of him yanked him down into the arms of sleep. He had to tell Pearl something, but both the words and the strength to speak eluded him and the next thing he saw was Beth's face, bloodied and twisted in pain.

27

I'm going down to help." Jim's long stride covered the distance between the window and the chair. Joe's weakened legs struggled to support his weight.

The big man dumped him onto the chair and was out the door before Joe could say or do anything more. A wagon had pulled into the driveway just as the big man had gotten him up. Two steps to the window and already he was feeling useless. He'd broken into a sweat just standing at the window, hanging on to the sill for support. Beth stopped the wagon in front of the house and gathered her skirts to climb down, but her foot caught and she sprawled onto the drive. He'd glimpsed blood.

From the chair where Jim had left him he could no longer see her. He pushed to the edge of the chair, feeling the beads of sweat that gathered on his upper lip. Jim's voice boomed from outside. Beth's reply soft. He relaxed. At least she was able to talk. Not hysterical and out of sorts by every little thing like Meredith. It was one more reason to love her.

Love . . .

He needed her, wanted to make sure she wasn't hurt, and had to wait until Jim could return. Joe chafed at his weakness, at the crutch that was across the room, at the dizziness that had him holding his head.

Pearl glided into the room. "Miss Beth had a fall. Jim sent me to—"

"She's bleeding."

"You saw?"

"From the window. Is she hurt?"

"Shaken." She grabbed the crutch from the corner and brought it to him. "Jim says you can use this to get yourself up. I'll help support your weight."

He did his best to lean more on the crutch than on Pearl. He took tiny steps, but each one required every ounce of concentration.

"Don't know what Jim is thinking, having you up so soon."

Joe inhaled deeply. His head throbbed from the effort, his muscles burned from disuse. She placed the cool cloth over his forehead. It felt so good he wanted to weep. That the woman could show him such kindness when he had been so . . . "I'm sorry if I scared you."

There was no response and he cracked an eye open. Pearl stood there, slack-jawed.

"Never had no white man ever tell me he was sorry."

"It's about time then, don't you think?"

———

Joe could stand it no longer. When Jim next entered the room, he demanded that the man take him to Beth.

"She still shook up from hitting her head."

But it had been a full day since her fall and he wanted to see for himself. To talk to her. "I miss her."

193

Jim's face split into a grin as broad as his shoulders. "Then we'll get you up." He handed over the crutch. "You lean on this and me."

The steps were tricky. Jim held tight to his good arm and he leaned his bad side against the wall.

Pearl appeared at the bottom of the staircase. "She right through here."

At the landing, he could see the whirl of activity. Anya spoke with three other women as they worked. She met his gaze and nodded, slipping a worried glance at the women. He took the warning and shuffled through to the parlor where Pearl motioned for him. His first sight of Beth sent his heart into a panicked gallop. She was pale and still. He shot forward, his feet moving as fast as he dared. Jim lunged to keep up.

"You best wake up and see this man," Jim's voice boomed.

Beth's eyes opened and she smiled into Joe's face as he lowered himself to the chair Pearl held for him.

"Are you feeling better?"

Her expression tightened. "I fell."

"I saw."

She squeezed her eyes shut and averted her face.

He leaned forward trying to understand her reaction. "I needed to make sure you were well." He touched her arm. "Bethie?"

She turned back to him, green eyes brimming with tears, cheeks flushed. "You're better. You're leaving."

He stilled, aware that Pearl and Jim both had retreated. "I'm stronger, yes, but . . ."

Her lips pressed together and a sob wracked her body. He slid his fingers down her arm, clasped her hand in his. "Beth, please . . . Are you in pain? Is your leg hurting?"

Another sob and still she would not look at him.

"Bethie."

"I wanted to be graceful and beautiful. Like Meredith."

He reached out to turn her face toward him. "Am I graceful and beautiful with my withered arm?"

"But . . . I fell."

Light began to dawn. "Do you fall a lot?"

An angry rush of red surged into her cheeks. She sniffed again. This meant more to her than he suspected. Her injury. The show of her embarrassment.

"I wanted to make sure you were well. Jim and I were standing at the window and I saw the blood."

"A cut." Her fingers brushed the spot where an abrasion targeted the place.

"My sister Sue fell a lot. She was always tripping over something."

Still, she would not look at him.

"Please leave me alone."

Jim came forward, and Joe wondered how much of the conversation the man had heard. "She is all right, isn't she?" he asked the big man as they retraced the steps toward the stairway.

"There is great heartache in Miss Beth. Her grandmother saw it, her parents saw it . . ."

28

Joe lay awake a good portion of the night, less because of the discomfort of the new bandage, more because he knew how troubled Beth was. Jim had helped him bathe before the bandage had been changed and he felt like a new man. Clean clothes, clean-shaven jaw, but the loose fit of the clothes showed him exactly how much work he had ahead of him to get better. Beth's mother had shown him the sizable chunk they'd removed from his shoulder, suspecting it was the culprit behind the wound's tendency to fester and the ebb and flow of his fevers.

Despite the strength he felt from the news and the pronouncement that his fever was much lower, and the exhaustion over the flurry of activity from his ablutions, he couldn't sleep. He'd opened his mouth several times to ask Anya about her daughter's limp, but he couldn't draw the courage to do so. Best for it to come from Beth herself.

When the bright morning light spilled onto the bed and warmed his face, Beth appeared. She approached him and touched his forehead and cheeks. "Mother said she thought the fever broke."

He caught her hand before she could withdraw. "God has answered my prayers."

Her face flushed and she tried to tug her hand fingers free from his grasp. "That's good news."

"I want to go for a walk."

"I'll get Jim."

"I want to go with you." He paused, not knowing how much strength he would have or how much distance he would be able to go before being forced to return to bed. But if he never tried, his strength would be reluctant to return, and he wanted to heal. For her. He stroked his thumb over the smooth back of her hand. "Tell me what has upset you." He'd debated the question most of the night. Her reluctance to talk of her limp, her embarrassment, all served to tell him something, and he thought he might know the problem. "Do you think it matters to me that you aren't graceful?"

Her lip quivered, then her jaw clenched. "It mattered to Riley."

His heart ached at the torn whisper of emotion in her voice. He kept his voice low. "Have you considered my arm? I'll never be the same. A very wise woman once told me that I had much to offer—love, life . . . Do you think she was wrong?"

The moment she raised her gaze to his, he knew she felt the gentle nudge of his words. "It's not the same."

"You're right. It's not. But it has left us both less than perfect in the eyes of others. Meredith wouldn't want me now and I'm glad of it. She was shallow and silly and I was a fool to think she wanted me for anything more than to rile her father."

Her eyes flew to his, her mouth opening, then closing.

His smile came slow, sure. "I think it shows a greater depth when someone can look beyond a body's weakness and see the beauty within, don't you, Bethie?"

She knew the answer. Wanted to believe that what he said was true. But Meredith aside, he was still leaving. He'd said so himself. How could she believe all that he said when words came easy but actions revealed those deeper recesses of the heart.

"Do you love me, Beth?"

She touched the tip of her tongue to her upper lip, frozen with fear. The answer sprang to her lips. So simple, but committing it to a single word weighed her with terror. She tugged her hand away and he released it. "I must go. Mother needs me. They are filling more wagons this morning."

She avoided looking into his face. There would be hurt there, but it would fade, just as her hurt had faded over Riley's rejection.

When she limped into the kitchen, her mother was alone working dough, perspiration beading along her forehead in the heat of the morning. Already she had done so much work. "What do you need me to do?"

Anya turned to her and smudged a hand over her cheek. "You could take over the kneading." She rubbed a hand over her shoulder and Beth knew her shoulder was stiffening up. They'd worked harder in the last few days and even their provisions were showing the sacrifice. But everyone was contributing and her parents would not do less. They were good-hearted people. Kind. Loving.

"Have you finished sewing your blocks?" Anya asked.

"I'm too tired to work on it in the evenings, and it seems such a selfish thing to indulge in something I enjoy doing when the soldiers need relief." Beth tried a smile. "No matter how hard I try, I fear I'll never forget how terrible it was."

Anya's flurry of activity stilled. She wiped her hand and turned, opening her arms. Beth went into them.

"You are whole and well, my daughter. God is in control even when it feels like the earth is shaking beneath us. You have begun to trust again. Don't let your trust be shaken because of things you cannot change."

She could not change the war, her limp, Leo's death, but, oh, how she wanted to. Yet through all of those circumstances Joe had come to her. If she'd married Riley, she would not have gone to be a nurse and met Joe.

Anya pulled back and studied her close. "How is your head this morning?"

"Fine."

"And your leg?"

"Stiff. Sore."

"Jim said Joe saw you, that you were upset by it."

She released a sigh and new tears burned her throat.

"He must care for you very much."

"Mother, please."

"Beth." Her mother's voice was firm and brooked no denial. "You cannot let Riley's rejection, Leo's death, your injury, rule your future."

She stiffened. "I have accepted God's hope."

"His hope for others, but for yourself?"

"I don't know what you mean."

Anya wiped her hands down the skirt of her apron. "God's hope is not just for eternity, but for here on Earth. For you and for me. Leo was granted the ultimate hope. Riley received his when he married Ava. But you have taken Leo's death and your injury more as a punishment than a path.

"We have watched you, and I committed to being silent on the matter, content to let God show you His will. But when I started seeing you drift farther and farther away I knew you had hardened your heart." She touched Beth's cheek. "You are so beautiful, yet you have allowed every bit of hope to be stolen from you for happiness here on Earth. Joe loves you."

She gasped.

"I have seen it in the way he watches you or perks up whenever your name is mentioned."

"But he's leaving."

"Do you love him?"

"I—I don't know."

"Then learn your heart but don't turn away from the hope."

Anya took a step back and pushed the trough of dough toward her. "If you'll finish this batch, Pearl should be back in time to do the next one. Perhaps you and Joe could spend some time talking."

She caught the little glance her mother shot her way and felt a lightening in her step as she set the trough on the table and sat down to work the dough. A sudden longing gripped her to work on the blocks, to see the richness of the colors of the triangles that led to that center point. Riley had moved on. Leo was content in heaven. She closed her eyes and let the warmth of the room penetrate the cold places of her heart as she worked the dough over and over. God was working her over just as she worked the dough, and the end result—that golden loaf of bread—would bring such comfort and nourishment to all who partook.

When Pearl and two neighbor ladies arrived in a wagon, she shared a glance with her mother, took off her apron, and slipped up the stairs. She reached the landing and rubbed her protesting leg just as the women swirled in on a stream of muted chatter and a rush of warm air.

She hesitated at Joe's door but continued down the hall. The blocks were spread on her bed, the bottom two rows almost complete, sewn as well as she could manage. Four more blocks remained to be attached, then the border. She drew her chair close to the window amazed at the thought that her mother thought Joe needed her. Loved her. She traced the outline of the bright golden square and smiled. She needed him too.

29

You have a plan to get me across?"

"We are close to the Potomac. It is deeper here, but there are ways."

Through the window and the thick leaves of sycamore and an occasional evergreen, he'd seen the sparkle of the river. From the house, the land sloped steeply down to the river in the distance. If he listened carefully, he could hear the water splashing over submerged rocks.

He didn't doubt Jim. Not at all. Only himself and his strength. If he overestimated what he was capable of and the current was more than he could handle. He shuddered.

"You will be safe. We will make sure of that for Miss Beth's sake."

He grinned. "For hers, but not for mine?"

"You are a Rebel." But Jim's shrug and shrewd smile showed how he teased.

"That makes me feel safe."

"We can always take you back into Sharpsburg," Jim said with verve.

Despite the lighthearted banter, he could not help but think of the fate of those men, his friends, left in the town now overrun with Union toops. God's mercy on him seemed unfair when he thought of what they would suffer. Yet he could not question God. He used different methods for different people, and Joe still had quite a few of his own obstacles to clear before he could leave, let alone come back.

He braced his leg against the crutch and closed his eyes against the sunshine. And how could he leave Beth?

"Walk back to me. Then we work on squeezing the ball."

Joe grimaced at the man. "I've already made three trips over there."

"You want to walk with Miss Beth?"

He did. They'd already talked of walking in the semidarkness, Jim nearby to help should he run into trouble and to keep an eye out for Union pickets patrolling the Potomac. All that the black man, that the family had done to keep him safe and well, amazed him. He froze up inside thinking about Beth. Leaving her would be hard, but he could never truly commit unless he left to set things straight.

The backs of his legs touched the mattress and he lowered himself to the soft comfort with a muffled groan as a knock came on the door. Jim opened it to a smiling Beth. She swept in, a dark bundle under her arm. Her eyes wavered between Joe and Jim, settling on Joe. She neither smiled nor frowned, but the sight of her choked his breath. "How could you, for one minute, think yourself inferior because of your leg?" His heart broke for her and for the self-deception that would work such a terrible trick in her mind.

He leaned forward and rose, ignored the jelly feel of his legs and used the crutch to close the distance between them. Jim scooted out the door, leaving the door open, as Beth's hand settled on his arm. "Maybe you should sit down. You look pale."

It took very little for him to see through her charade. "You never answered my question."

Her mouth opened. He leaned forward and pressed his lips to her forehead. "I want to come back to you. But I have to do it the right way. For my conscience. For Ben."

"What if you don't find out what happened to him?" She stared at the buttons on his shirt.

"Then I will rest in the knowledge that I tried." He let the silence grow. "Who hurt you, Beth? Your injury doesn't bother me."

"You've not seen me walk. I . . ."

He touched her jaw, raised her chin. "But I have. I still love you."

She lowered her eyes and tried to turn her face away but he kept gentle hold on her chin.

"If you don't love me, Bethie, then I'm going to come back and make you love me. You can't get rid of me so easily."

He meant it. Yet, she'd seen sincerity before, in Riley's eyes, and it had morphed into something else entirely when he had realized her leg would never heal.

Joe released her chin and took a wobbly step backward. He turned, using the crutch in an awkward pivot that nearly sent him to the floor. "I'll never get used to using this thing."

"It will only be for a while."

He was letting the subject drop and she felt grateful that he did not press her for an answer. Still, she could not deny the warmth that spilled through her at hearing those three words, at his assurance that she would be enough for him despite her leg.

"What do you have there?"

It took her a minute to understand what he meant. His amused nod toward the bundle beneath her arm made her laugh. She shook out the blocks, careful to set aside the last three that needed to be sewn. He fingered the material.

"When we're married, I want this for our room."

Her face went hot. She dared to glance at him and her face flushed even hotter when she caught his mischievous grin.

"You're lovely when you blush."

"Joe . . . this isn't appropriate."

The bed squeaked as he shifted forward. "You're right. We'll save it for another time."

Despite herself, a wave of pleasure rolled through her at the thought that he could even find her attractive enough to make such an intimate tease.

Joe coaxed several blushes from Beth during their evening walks. Jim always lingered nearby. On the fourth night, Joe went without the crutch, not minding in the least when Beth stayed extra close, her anxious expression all concern for him.

Green eyes stared into his. "Have I told you how beautiful you are today?"

The hot blush had her drawing back, averting her face, and he chuckled as they continued toward the edge of the thick woods. His goal to increase his distance every day had been measured by both Jim and Beth. Though meeting the goals brought pleasure, it also dampened his spirits. For each day that slipped past meant he was closer to the time he would need to leave.

Beth brushed against his shoulder with each step of her left leg and he savored both her nearness and the reminder of her imperfection. Meredith's perfection sickened him. Her superficial airs and shallow personality, but every moment with Beth only deepened his love and admiration for the slight woman. He placed his hand over her cool fingers. In the next step, she jarred and twisted away from him. She was falling but he caught her around the waist and shifted her weight to him.

She choked out a gasp.

"Are you hurt? What happened."

"I—there was a hole."

He steadied her on her feet as she leaned to massage her knee. "We should head back."

She didn't respond. Didn't look at him.

"Beth?" Her sniff was his first clue. She wiped at her face and he pulled her close and cradled her head against him. "Bethie, don't cry."

Her tears were not a torrent, but a trickle. When he pulled back, she still would not meet his eyes.

"Look at me." He tried to lift her chin but she pulled away.

"This is what it's like. I'm never ever the graceful woman that can—"

He put his hands on her shoulders. "Stop it, Bethie. Stop it. This coming from a woman holding the dead arm of a soldier."

"It moves now. It's stronger."

"But it's not quite right. What do I have to do to convince you that your injury doesn't matter to me? It's you I love. The woman caught inside a beautiful shell with a leg that doesn't work quite as well as it did because she sacrificed herself while trying to help another."

"Riley stopped loving me."

"Then he's a fool. A shallow fool and I'll tell him to his face."

Her head tilted and her eyes searched his, great wells of water filling her eyes. She blinked and tears spilled down her cheeks. He smudged them away with his thumbs, tilted her head back. "No more of that. It hurts me to hear you think less of yourself."

⚬⚬⚬

Gazing into his eyes, seeing the tenseness of his expression, hearing his words, Beth knew she had to stop the fear. To believe herself lovable and Joe capable of loving her. As much as she prayed for God to help her, the moment of truth had come. She could choose to take another step toward the hope, or retreat to the darkness. "I'm sorry."

He crushed her in a hug that left her breathless, yet cherished. She squeezed out a laugh and elbowed him away. "Keep walking, soldier. You haven't gone the whole way yet."

"Only if you'll go with me."

He tried to hold out his right arm. She rested her hand on his, feeling the thinness of the limb. Muscle had developed, but she knew Joe's frustration stemmed from the slowness with which his muscles responded.

"Now, tell me how many children you'd like to have."

Heat surged into her cheeks. "Joseph Madison!"

He put on an innocent expression that melted into something else entirely. He stopped her, drew her close. "If only you could see the woman I see."

Her heart slammed hard, and she wondered if he knew how much his words meant. How she would hang on to them in the days ahead of inevitable loneliness. She lifted her hands to his neck, touched the hair that skimmed the collar of his shirt, lifted on her toes to press her lips against his cheek. "Thank you."

His arm snaked around her back. "I'd rather hear something else."

She put her lips against his ear. "I love you, Joe."

30

Joe wanted to hang on to every minute of every day that he could spend with Beth. Watching her joy over his recovery made him reluctant to leave. A dozen times he had made up his mind to stay, but he would take out that stiff piece of paper and the cigar he was sure Ben had left in his haversack, and he knew he needed to at least try and make sense of Ben's actions and sudden death. Besides, he could not desert. Could not live his life running. Sometimes he caught Beth with the same heart-twisting sadness in her eyes that he felt as each evening's good-night marked another day's passing.

Jedidiah's return came three weeks after the Union took over Sharpsburg. Anya's sudden appearance in the open doorway of Joe's room, her mouth pinched with anxiousness, said more than the booming voice of Beth's father greeting someone.

"I thought I should warn you." Anya's mouth curved into a smile. "I know if he will talk to you, he will come to love you as we have."

Joe braced his hands on the arms of the chair they'd brought into his room to push to a stand. Beth was already on her feet. "You don't have to—"

But Joe captured her hand. "I will not hide. Not if you are to become my bride."

She opened her mouth, then clamped it shut again. Anya led the way down the hallway. Joe could hear the unfamiliar voice that sounded so much like Nicklaus's but different, too.

Nicklaus moved forward as Joe reached the landing. Beth stood beside him, her nervousness apparent in the stiffness with which she met her brother's enthusiastic hug.

Jedidiah's gaze finally settled on him. He could see the man measuring him, a question in his eyes. He held out his hand. "I'm Joe Madison."

Nicklaus moved forward. He clamped a hand on Joe's shoulder, then Jed's. "He's a soldier your grandmother and sister took care of during Sharpsburg."

Jed's strong features and broad chest made up for his relative shortness. He stared between them. "I tried to find grandma but . . ."

"She's gone," Beth inserted into the heavy silence. "She worked so hard to take care of all the soldiers the Confederates brought to us. The Union, too." Joe heard the catch in her voice.

Joe held out his hand to the man. "I am sorry for your grandmother's death. But she took good care of me, just as she hoped someone would care for you if you were wounded and in the South."

Jed gripped his hand hard, the words penetrating and revealing Joe's secret. Joe decided to have it all out there. He would not leave Nicklaus to defend him; he would meet Jedidiah's disapproval head-on. He released Jed's hand.

"Beth has spoken often of you, and has worried at your reaction to our . . . affections. Whether you approve or not, I cannot help but love her." Beth's hand slipped into his.

Nicklaus squeezed his shoulder, as Jedidiah searched Beth's face. A flare of anger surged, then faded to be replaced by chagrin. A smile broke through. Relief seemed to swirl through the air. Jed pulled Beth into his arms and whispered something against her ear that made her gasp. And, finally, Jed worked Joe's hand up and down. "Welcome to the family, brother."

Only later, after they ate a hearty meal and Jed mounted a scrawny horse to head back to Sharpsburg, did Joe find out Jed's secret. He and Beth sat on the porch step in the fading light of day, he sitting in the darker shadows where he could not be so easily seen, she in the rocking chair with the quilt blocks spread on her lap. She was working on sewing one of the last two. Just watching her silhouette stirred his joy and tumbled his emotions. So much like those days during the battle when she had sat next to him and sewed. They had shared so little, yet so very much.

"What did Jed tell you, Beth?"

She shot him a glance filled with good humor as she pulled the needle through and the thread taut. "He told me he was in love with a Southern woman."

Joe bent a knee and draped his arm across it, shaking his head as he chuckled. "Worry comes so easy, and then God smooths things out and we wonder why we worried at all." Beth didn't comment. When he glanced at her, her downcast eyes told him she was battling her worries again. He scooted from the shadows, closer to the light until he could look up into her face and see the traces of the silver tears along her cheeks.

"Bethie . . ." He went up on his knees and gathered her close.

"I've tried all day not to cry."

Me too, he wanted to say but for a very different reason.

"Jim told you it's time, didn't he?"

He sat back on his heels. He should have known she had overheard his conversation with Jim the previous evening. She had gone inside for coffee and Jim had appeared from the barn to whisper to him the plans made to get him across the Potomac. Roy would help, as would Pearl. But when Jim had slipped away and Joe had turned, she'd been standing there.

"Yes," he braced his arm against the back of the rocker, hoping to ease the reality of what he would say. "He did."

Already her eyes were wet, though she fought the tears. "When?"

He swallowed. He'd done his best to shove aside the thoughts of his looming departure. So much sooner than he wanted it to be. He swallowed, caught her gaze, begging for her understanding, wishing so much it was already done and he didn't have to go away at all. "Tomorrow night."

She squeezed her eyes shut.

He sat back and covered her hand with his, careful to avoid getting stuck in the fabric. Her fingers felt cool against his hand, but it was a perfect fit. There would be dark days ahead and he didn't know when he'd be able to return, though Jim had mentioned a way Joe could communicate when he was ready to come North again. He had given a list of names, slaves most likely. Relatives? He didn't ask, only committed the names to memory and promised to protect the information. "They will get the message to me," Jim had assured him. Joe's throat had burned with gratitude over the man's help. "They know of your sacrifice for Roy, Jonah, and Pearl. They will do what they can to help you in return."

But now, here, as time ticked off with every sweep of the cold breeze and tick of the grandfather clock . . . he'd thought about it long and hard. He needed so much to take something with him to remind him of Beth. Something to offer him comfort and hope. His request would sound strange to most, but she would understand. "I want to take the last block with me, Beth."

Her brows drew together. "Block?"

"The last quilt block. It's my symbol of comfort and hope. It reminds me that God cares, of my love for you and yours for me. And," it was harder to talk now but he pressed on. "The quilt will forever remain unfinished until that last block is brought home again. We'll both be incomplete without each other and the quilt—"

His voice caught and his eyes filled.

In slow motion, she released his hand and used the block to touch away the moisture fading down his cheeks, even as tears spilled down her own. In the silence, she spread the block out again and made slow work of folding it into a small square. It seemed such a small thing. So inconsequential in the face of what he felt for her. He stroked the hair back from her face and smiled his promise into her eyes.

Epilogue

Eighteen Months Later, Beth's Journal

At first there were no letters from Joe. I did my best to be patient, knowing the war raged on, but my imagination sometimes spun out of control and I would seek out my mother to pray with me, over me. After six months, Roy brought a packet of envelopes to me. I didn't ask and he didn't offer any explanation, only that smile that seemed so much like Jim's— secretive but sure.

The stack held five letters from Joe, and he promised more. He wrote of missing me, of his adventures, of securing his discharge, of his visit to his home that was no longer there. My heart ached for all he endured and I wondered about Ben, if Joe had found out anything. None of the letters said anything of that.

After those letters, I received nothing else. I wanted so much to ask Roy if he should check or talk to Jim, but I was afraid to compromise whatever communications the blacks might have. I had to trust them. How strong I had wanted to be in Joe's love, but his lingering absence and the lack of letters gnawed at me as surely as a rat gnawed at a sack of grain. Not a day went by that I didn't pray for strength to believe in his promise of hope.

I worked harder than ever, sewing quilts for the men and visiting the few field hospitals still in operation after Sharpsburg. Slowly, things were becoming more normal. Then, one night, my mother came to my room, a smile on her face. She motioned me to follow her and I did, hope growing with each step as the hum of voices greeted me. I descended the steps to find Roy, Jim, and Pearl standing with my father, and in the center, Joe. My heart beat so hard I thought I might faint but when he caught me and twirled me around, when I saw the emotion brimming in his eyes and felt the slam of his heart against mine, I knew my wait was over.

He said nothing, couldn't, for we were too busy crying, savoring our togetherness. I touched the hair that had grown long against his neck. He rocked me, his face buried in my hair, saying all the words I'd longed to hear again. When Joe finally pulled back, he led me to the porch where his haversack lay amid a bundle of other things and we would have privacy. He settled me in the rocking chair. We couldn't stop smiling at each other. He lifted out two things, the cigar and the piece of paper, and sat across from me.

"Ben?"

His expression went sober. He nodded.

"You didn't write of him. I wondered . . ."

"It was too dangerous to write about but, now, I can tell you." He smoothed the back of his hand down my cheek. I laughed from the sheer excitement of having him near again and it was another few minutes before Joe could settle back to the objects and his explanation.

"General Lee wrote out his commands to his generals outlining his plan. But one copy was lost. Special Order 191 was found in a field by a Union corporal named Mitchell." He shifted his weight and I couldn't help noticing how much better he was able to move his right arm. Not perfect but far better than those first days . . . "Ben and I were bivouacked in that field, and he said something to me the night before we left, that things were going to get better soon." He raked a hand through his hair. "I don't know if he had anything to do with it. I'll never know, but the paper," he pointed to the sheet, "has the same watermark found on the order, and the cigar . . ."

He raised his head and gave me a sad look. "It tore me up pretty bad to think he would be involved in something of that nature, but Ben was tore up as much as me, as anyone, over Sue and Mama. I could see why he would feel compelled to do something so desperate."

"Who shot him? Why?"

He shook his head. "I don't quite know." I knew a mantle of weariness would always hang over him at the question mark of what happened to his brother. "If someone found him out, it makes sense he would be shot. But I'll never know, Beth, and I prefer to look forward rather than backward."

I held Joe's hand and stroked his knuckles. He gave me a little nod of reassurance and turned his hand in mine so that our palms met. It was time to change the subject. To talk about us. I blushed at the intensity of his gaze.

"Your arm has grown stronger."

He glanced at his arm, at our joined hands, pleased with my comment. "Not quite right, but better." He released my hand to pluck something else from the haversack. Dark and worn and soft. The quilt block. He handed it to me. "Now you can finish that quilt." A spark lit his eyes that stole my breath. "We'll need it to keep us warm this winter."

Discussion Questions

1. Was Beth's perception of herself healthy? How did this perception affect her spiritually?

2. What do you think Beth's parents saw in her that worried them so much following Beth's injury and the death of Leo?

3. Gerta's opinionated nature ostracized her to some extent in her town. Do you know someone whose tendency and quickness to express his or her opinion often lands that person in hot water? Do you admire this type of person? What advice would you give this person?

4. Gerta's attitude was to help all those she could. Beth was more determined to help Union soldiers only. What changed Beth's attitude? What would you do if you were faced with such a situation?

5. Gerta believed that by giving the Confederate soldiers food willingly it would deter them from taking it by force and possibly taking their revenge on the women. Do you believe this was a wise choice? What other solution would you offer?

6. How does being caught in the middle of the war help mature Beth's opinion of herself and her lame leg?

7. Joe lost everything he held dear before and during the war. How would such losses affect your desire to continue fighting? Do you think his attitude toward the war was justified?

8. Beth and Joe spent many long hours waiting out the cannonading of the town, Beth trying to help Gerta, Joe flat on his back because of his injury. Which do you think would be harder to endure: the activity and seeing all the terrible sights Beth saw or the hours of forced inactivity?

9. Beth's mother tried to help her daughter understand the darkness in her heart through the quilt. As a parent, have you ever tried to relay a silent message to your child in hopes they will one day understand the deeper meaning? Did it work?

10. Jim is a pivotal secondary character with a huge heart to help those he befriends, doing much of his good deeds without thought or regard for himself. Do you know someone with such a sacrificial nature? What do you do to show your appreciation to them?

11. Though Beth's home is fictional, the Piper farm was real and commandeered by Longstreet during the Battle of Antietam. How do you think you would react if war came to your doorstep? What preparation would you make for you and your family?

12. Though only mentioned in the ending, the loss of Lee's Special Order 191 was critical to the victory of McClellan at Antietam. Before this story, had you ever heard that Lee "lost" such an important document preceding the Battle of Antietam?

Want to learn more about author
S. Dionne Moore and check out other great
fiction from Abingdon Press?

Sign up for our fiction newsletter at
www.AbingdonPress.com
to read interviews with your favorite authors, find tips
for starting a reading group, and stay posted on what
new titles are on the horizon. It's a place to connect
with other fiction readers or post a
comment about this book.

Be sure to visit S. Dionne online!

http://www.sdionnemoore.com

We hope you enjoyed *A Heartbeat Away* and that you will continue to read the Quilts of Love series of books from Abingdon Press. Here's an excerpt from the next book in the series, Bonnie S. Calhoun's *Pieces of the Heart.*

—∞—

Pieces of the Heart
Bonnie S. Calhoun

1

June 15, 1938

Corde-eel-ee, don't be sil-ly. We'll find you sooner or later!"

The taunt echoed down the alley, bouncing from building to building, at the same rate as her heartbeat pounded in her ears. The voices pumped more adrenaline into her blood. Would they pop into the Court from Pine Street?

Cordelia Grace pedaled her red and tan Schwinn as fast as her legs would go. She sucked in short rapid breaths that burned her lungs. She took a glance behind. No one. She swerved, avoiding the metal garbage cans in front of Stoney's Garage. Panic raced through her throat as tears pricked at her eyes. Where were her two girlfriends? They were supposed to be right behind her. Now she was alone to face her tormentors.

She probably wouldn't have run from them if she had "more meat on her bones" like Grammy said. Other girls had the weight and power she lacked. Why did she have to fight? Truth be told . . . she didn't know *how* to fight. Her daddy was a preacher man, and her mama always said young ladies of good breeding didn't act like street hoodlums. No one ever taught her self-defense.

She breathed hard, pulling in big gulps of air. Maybe they hadn't seen her turn down Dix Court? Maybe she could make it home safely . . . today. The alley, wide enough for cars to pass in either direction, felt as though it were closing in on her, squeezing her into the dusty center. She prayed someone would be on their porch. Just one grown-up she could stop and talk with until the danger passed. But each house stood silent, each narrow porch empty. Rows of garbage cans lined impossibly narrow strips of grass like tin soldiers, but none offered protection.

The quarter-sized scab on her left knee caught on the hem of her play dress as her legs pumped the pedals. The tiny prickle pains from the pulled skin would be worth it if she managed to escape. She jerked her head around to look back again. Long skinny braids whacked her in the face and slapped her in the right eye. Tears spilled onto her cheek. Bitsy Morgan's house marked the halfway point in the alley. Still no one in hot pursuit.

Her arms relaxed on the handlebars and her legs slowed. She back-pedaled to brake. The bicycle slid to a stop. Cordelia hopped off the seat, her legs straddling the "J" frame. Her lungs burned.

Five houses up, they emerged on the path leading to the avenue. The three bullies spread across the court, blocking her way.

Cordelia whimpered as dread clenched her belly. They found her. She tried to turn but the chain caught her dress hem, wrenching the handlebars from her grip. The bicycle fell and the chain dug into the soft flesh of her ankle. A trail of black grease tracked down her white sock. Ignore the pain. If they see tears, they'll know I'm scared. She lifted her quivering chin and stared.

Two girls and a boy ran at her.

She bent over and raised her bicycle.

Two more girls raced toward her. The five Wilson kids trapped their prey. She tried not to let fear register in her eyes.

"Cor-deel-lee, you belong to me." Debbie Lu, the taller girl in the group, had her nappy hair pulled back in a short pony-tail so tight it pulled back the corners of her eyes, adding to her sinister look.

Cordelia shrank back, choking her handlebars with shaking hands. She watched the Wilson girl approach, slapping her fist into the palm of her other hand.

Debbie Lu charged and slammed into Cordelia with the full force of both fists.

Cordelia stumbled from her bicycle and skidded to the ground. Her palms raked over the graveled dirt of the alley. The sting forced tears into her eyes. She refused to respond.

A red flash streaked from the roof of the shed on the left side of the alley. A cute light-skinned boy landed on the ground beside her bicycle. He wore blue jeans and a bright red shirt opened down the front revealing a dingy T-shirt. Cordelia eyed him warily, another tormentor.

He didn't join the bullies.

She looked him up and down. Who was he? Her heart pounding eased.

The cute boy stepped between her and Debbie Lu. "What's the problem?" He thumbed back at Cordelia. "Did she steal your Tootsie Pop?"

"I'm gonna pop her all right. Little Miss High Yella' doesn't belong in this neighborhood with her light skin and good hair. She acts like she's white people and better'n us," said the dark-complexioned girl.

The cute boy turned away from Debbie Lu to glance at Cordelia.

Cordelia froze.

He raised one side of his lips in a slight smile and winked, then turned back to the menace. "In case you haven't noticed, you should probably call me high yella' too since my skin is as light as hers. Does that mean you want me out of the neighborhood, too?" He stepped closer to the girl. "See, I just moved here, and I don't think my pa would want to leave, since he just got a job at the coal company."

The girl scowled but lowered her fist and backed up.

Tim Wilson, the brother of the group, pushed Debbie Lu out of the way and stood toe-to-toe with the new boy. "Don't you talk to my sister like that."

"Or what?" The cute boy's eyebrows furrowed and he lowered his head a tad.

Cordelia eyed the exchange. Her brain told her to run while she had the chance, but her feet stayed rooted to the spot. What did he think he was doing facing off with the Wilson kids? They were well-known scrappers.

Tim Wilson raised his left hand.

The cute boy's right fist shot out and punched Tim square in the nose.

Tim's hands cupped his nose as blood squirted down the front of his shirt and splattered his sisters.

The girls screamed. Both hightailed it down the alley.

Cordelia grimaced. An involuntary sigh pushed from her chest. This boy wasn't afraid of them.

"I'll get you for this," Tim warned in a nasal tone.

"Yeah, well, when you're not bleeding and wanna stop playing house with your sisters, be sure and let me know."

Tim pointed a bloody finger at the boy. "Hey, you take that back or I'm gonna beat your—"

"Oh, no! I'm sorry," the cute boy interrupted, his voice pleading. "I didn't mean to hurt you."

Cordelia's heart sank. So much for her fearless hero. She couldn't blame him, but somehow it felt worse than Debbie Lu's fist in her belly.

Which way should she run before Tim called his sisters back to finish the job?

The boy added, "Yeah, I'm sorry. I meant to hit your sister."

Tim scowled through the mess dripping from his chin. He sputtered, but before he could speak, Cordelia's rescuer faked a lunge. Tim recoiled with a girlish squeal and sprang after his sisters.

Cordelia's eyes widened as she stared at the back of the cute boy's head.

He turned to face her. "Do you talk?"

She hadn't spoken a single word to her surprise hero. A nervous smile crossed her lips. Her dry throat croaked out the word. "Yes." She swallowed hard and wet her lips. "Thank you for helping me." A flutter settled into her tummy.

He looked down at the mess of blood on his own sleeve. With a look of disgust he ripped the shirt off and threw it to the ground. A rolled up tube of paper fell from his back pocket. "Jeepers creepers, I gotta lose that. If my ma sees blood on my shirt I'm gonna be in real big trouble for fightin' again."

Cordelia smiled. "I could explain for you. You were very brave—"

"No! Pa told me if I got in trouble in this town, he was gonna . . ." He kicked at the shirt. He locked his fingers together over his head, resting his arms against his ears. "I'll run away before . . ."

Cordelia tipped her head to the side to look up into his downcast eyes. "Before what?"

He mumbled.

"What did you say?"

He looked defiant. "I said before I get beat again."

Cordelia jerked back her chin at the odd choice of words.

"Berr-nard!" The voice carried over the fence.

"Com-ing," he yelled but never took his eyes off Cordelia.

His stare reached into her soul. She shivered. He looked about thirteen. Same age as her, but at least a head taller, and really cute. He'd be gone in a second. Cordelia's heart thumped an erratic rhythm. At least she knew his name . . . Bernard.

"I have to go before she comes looking for me. My dad will be home from the mines any minute. I got to already be at the dinner table when he comes in." He reached for the rickety wooden gate.

"Hey, you dropped something." Cordelia pointed at the rolled paper.

Bernard grabbed it up and unrolled the tube. Flattened, he showed her the comic book with a mostly yellow and white cover. A man in blue tights and a red cape lifted a car over his head. "This is the first Action Comic! And this here is Superman. He flies over tall buildings."

Cordelia looked at the page, then back at Bernard. "So what?"

He just shook his head. "So what? Do you know how many extra chores I had to do for the ten cents to buy this?" He shook his head. "You're just a girl. Girls know nothin'."

She tipped her head to the side and a smile creased her lips. "Well, can you fly and lift a car over your head?" He used what she considered super-human strength to save her. Her regular smart-alecky mouth replaced her anxiety. Grammy said her mouth always got her in trouble. She wanted to slap herself for being flippant.

He began to argue.

"Berr-nard, dinn-ner," a lady's voice yelled from the other side of the tall wooden fence.

He never took his eyes off Cordelia. "Comin', Ma!"

He turned to the gate, and then back to Cordelia. "What's your name, girl?"

"Cordelia . . . Cordelia Grace." Now her heart pounded for a different reason.

"Good to meet you, Cordelia-Cordelia Grace. He winked and reached for the gate.

"Welcome to the neighborhood." Cordelia's heart thumped against her ribs. Her voice trailed off as the gate closed behind him.

Cordelia leaned over and grabbed up the red shirt. She held it up, looking for the spots of blood. Scrunching up her nose, she folded the splashes to the inside. Why did she want this messy thing? She stuffed the shirt into the book bag in her bicycle basket. Then pedaled out of the alley and down Olive Street.

May 19, 1942

"Did you hear what I asked you, baby girl?"

Cordelia's thoughts jerked back to the present but her hand rested on the red circle of triangles. The memory both stung and warmed her heart. "I'm sorry. What did you ask, Grammy?"

"Well, I asked what had you deep in thought. You even breathed heavy for a spell there." Grammy Mae measured squares of colored cloth as she rocked in her chair.

Cordelia hitched up the side of her mouth in a wry smile. "Ya know how some people can pinpoint when their lives changed for the better or worse?"

"Yes, baby. I've heard tell about folks like that. For me, I just personally felt it all began the day I was birthed." Grammy Mae, with her hair pulled back in a perfect chignon, wore a tailored house dress, and looked prim and proper every day Cordelia could remember. Even her black Hill and Dale stack heel oxfords were polished to a high shine. Grammy loved shoes. She taught Cordelia the brand name of every pair, though to her grandmother's chagrin, Cordelia preferred to go barefoot.

Cordelia rubbed her hand over the red material close to the center of the quilt. "Well this is when I was reborn."

Grammy smiled. "I knew the day you brought that bloody shirt in here, something was burnin' in your belly."

"That day I met Bernard." She sighed remembering the whole jumble of feelings. Her mind had raced to find excuses for the dirt on her play dress. She didn't want to tell about being pushed to the ground. A bicycle fall always seemed a handy excuse. Sometimes she was sure Grammy guessed the truth. And then there was her Superman, Bernard Howard.

Cordelia knew they were destined to marry, from the moment she laid eyes on him and stole his cast-off shirt. "That day you started my quilt, too. I feel different now than when I was thirteen. How could that be a whole four years ago?"

Different wasn't exactly the right word. She still feared being deserted, and she was still very good at hiding her dirty secret about God. Older, yes. A more appropriate definition.

She looked up. "Do you think someone my age could be in love?"

Grammy stroked Cordelia's hair. "Well, of course, child. In my day, girls close to your age were already married and birthing babies. You've got a good head on your shoulders. You know your mind."

"Seems like only yesterday." Grammy continued to rock and cut squares. "Out of all the boys skulking around here at the time, why did you pick up with him?"

Cordelia knew all too vividly why Bernard became her hero, but this was not the time to speak her personal pain out loud. "Because I was worried over something he said that day about his father."

Grammy looked up from the pile of colored squares resting in her lap. "What did he say?"

"He said his father beat him." Those words made her hands shake after all these years.

Grammy Mae stopped rocking.

"And he said he was going to run away if he got beat again. I didn't understand why he would he make such a big deal outta getting switched. Daddy always made me go out back to the willow tree and cut my own. That part was worse than getting hit, but I never thought of running away."

Actually a switching usually consisted of more threat than action. She could only remember getting whacked a couple times. She'd learned an instant performance of crying and screaming, regardless of how light the whack, would cause her father to relent.

Grammy Mae looked like a storm cloud was fixing to bust from her forehead. "I don't think the boy was talking about a regular switchin' baby. I think he could have been talking about a full-on man beatin'."

Cordelia nodded. "That's what I found out later. His father is a real nightmare. But he wouldn't try to beat him like that now because Bernard swears he'd fight back."

Grammy set her jaw.

Cordelia knew that look well. She needed to change topics before Grammy took off to Dix Court to punch Mr. Howard in the eye or worse. "Tell me the story of my life covering again."

Cordelia glanced around the room at the piles of colored squares spread across the dressing table, ironing board, and bedspread. Over these past four years, the circular Pine Cone Quilt pattern had grown to several feet in circumference.

Grammy's look softened. "Baby girl, I've told you the story of this quilt a dozen times. You should be able to recite it by heart."

"But I like to hear you say it." Actually, she enjoyed seeing the twinkle in Grammy's eyes as she talked.

Grammy Mae looked up, smiled, and then nodded her head. "I guessed it was up to me to teach you since the tradition goes back as many generations as I can remember on our side of the family. This is a Pine Cone Quilt. Some folks on my daddy's side of the family call it a Pine Burr Quilt, but it all works out to be the same pattern."

"You started working on it because Mom didn't like it."

"Now, Cordelia. Don't be startin' no trouble with your Ma. I started your quilt because it was time someone got to work on it," said Grammy with a hint of annoyance in her voice. "It's not that she didn't like it. She didn't think it was necessary to give you a life covering."

Grammy and Ma were always at odds about the ways of the world. Ma called herself modern. Cordelia had caught her more than once mocking Grammy for talking about the olden days.

Her father told her their tussles resulted from two women, only related by marriage, of different generations in the same house. Grammy was Daddy's mom. She liked to say she came from different stock than Ma's family. Sometimes Cordelia felt the tension between her ma and Grammy, but for the most part the two women stayed out of each other's way. Cordelia pretended to not pay much attention. But she adored Grammy, her confidant and ally.

Cordelia grinned. "She doesn't know how to quilt either."

"Baby girl, hush your mouth. The youngsters don't do a lot of the things we learned as girls. Now, let me tell the story."

Cordelia stifled a giggle at the thought of her mother navigating anything more complicated than the sales aisle at Woolworths.

Grammy reached across and pulled folded muslin material into her lap. She shook it out across her knees. Concentric circles spaced about an inch and a half apart, spread from the edge of the large completed circle.

"Our family tradition holds that the quiltmaker prays over each square, folding prayers into the triangles." Grammy grabbed up a square. She folded it diagonally once to form a triangle, then folded each outside point in to create a square.

She held out the piece of green gingham material. "See this? I just folded in a prayer for your good health as I made the corners."

Cordelia fingered the square and glanced across the pile of cut pieces. "Where'd you get all this material?"

"From clothes that don't fit you any more or special pieces of fabric I think you'll want to remember. They're your life moments, you know."

Grammy rocked softly as she measured and cut the squares with a large pair of sharp sewing shears. "Going back through the generations, each young lady is presented with her life covering on her eighteenth birthday. It's the prayers, dreams, and wishes spoken for her and her life as a woman, wife, and mother. I was determined no granddaughter of mine was going without her own covering."

Cordelia fingered some of the squares. "Can I get yours out of the trunk?"

"Yes, baby, you may. I declare, as much as you fondle that old thing, you're going to rub all the colors off."

Cordelia lifted the lid of the steamer trunk at the foot of Grammy Mae's bed and sorted through several layers of clothing to find it. The bold colors drew the usual gasp of pleasure from Cordelia. "Oh Grammy, every time I look at this I think it gets more beautiful! Are you sure I couldn't have yours?"

"No, baby, every girl gets her own special one. These are the blessings for my life. You'll get your own blessings. I explained to you about Elijah and Elisha. Each had his own mantle. This one is yours." Grammy touched the quilt she was making. "You take care of your quilt, and it will take care of you."

"But your colors are quite beautiful."

"Those were clothes I wore when I was a youngster. Yours will have colors and prayers special just for you. It will be ready when you're eighteen."

Cordelia lifted her head to look at Grammy. "It seems like forever to get to eighteen."

Grammy Mae tipped back her head and laughed. "It's only a year away."

QUILTS *of* LOVE

EVERY QUILT HAS A STORY

There is a strong connection between storytelling and quilts. Like a favorite recollection, quilts are passed from one generation to the next as precious heirlooms. They bring communities together.

The Quilts of Love series focuses on women who have woven romance, adventure, and even a little intrigue into their own family histories. Featuring contemporary and historical romances as well as occasional light mystery, this series will draw you into uplifting, heartwarming, exciting stories of characters you won't soon forget.

Visit **QuiltsofLoveBooks.com** for more information.

For more information and for more
fiction titles, please visit
AbingdonPress.com/fiction.

Abingdon Press fiction
a novel approach to faith

What They're Saying About...

The Glory of Green, by Judy Christie
"Once again, Christie draws her readers into the town, the life, the humor, and the drama in Green. *The Glory of Green* is a wonderful narrative of small-town America, pulling together in tragedy. A great read!"
—Ane Mulligan, editor of *Novel Journey*

Always the Baker, Never the Bride, by Sandra Bricker
"[It] had just the right touch of humor, and I loved the characters. Emma Rae is a character who will stay with me. Highly recommended!"
—Colleen Coble, author of *The Lightkeeper's Daughter* and the *Rock Harbor* series

Diagnosis Death, by Richard Mabry
"Realistic medical flavor graces a story rich with characters I loved and with enough twists and turns to keep the sleuth in me off-center. Keep 'em coming!"—**Dr. Harry Krauss, author of *Salty Like Blood* and *The Six-Liter Club***

Sweet Baklava, by Debby Mayne
"A sweet romance, a feel-good ending, and a surprise cache of yummy Greek recipes at the book's end? I'm sold!"—**Trish Perry, author of *Unforgettable* and *Tea for Two***

The Dead Saint, by Marilyn Brown Oden
"An intriguing story of international espionage with just the right amount of inspirational seasoning."—*Fresh Fiction*

Shrouded in Silence, by Robert L. Wise
"It's a story fraught with death, danger, and deception—of never knowing whom to trust, and with a twist of an ending I didn't see coming. Great read!"—**Sharon Sala, author of *The Searcher's Trilogy: Blood Stains, Blood Ties,* and *Blood Trails*.**

Delivered with Love, by Sherry Kyle
"Sherry Kyle has created an engaging story of forgiveness, sweet romance, and faith reawakened—and I looked forward to every page. A fun and charming debut!"—**Julie Carobini, author of *A Shore Thing* and *Fade to Blue*.**

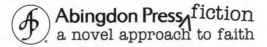

Abingdon Press fiction
a novel approach to faith

AbingdonPress.com | 800.251.3320

BKM112220003 PACP01034642-01